TRAITORS

Two weeks to live. Three lives to take.
One chance to uncover the truth before time runs out.

First published in paperback by
Michael Terence Publishing in 2025
www.mtp.agency

ISBN 9781805880264

Cover design (AI)
Michael Terence Publishing

Michael Terence
Publishing

Acknowledgements

An enormous thanks to my proof reader and grammar corrector guru Pat Johns for the many hours of painstaking work she contributed to this book.

My thanks also to Rachel Wicks of Electric Footprint for her encouragement and invaluable social media expertise.

Finally to the fantastic team at Michael Terence Publishing, in particular to Karolina Robinson for her creative ideas and cover design and to Keith Abbott who yet again patiently and expertly guided me through all the various stages of actually bringing this book to publication.

This book is dedicated to the staff of Whipps Cross Hospital, particularly the specialist nurses in the urology department who have constantly demonstrated their expertise, patience and friendly care to myself and others. Thank you Ladies, you are doing an absolutely fantastic job.

In memory of James Goldsmith (1897-1982) my grandfather who had such a positive influence on my life.

Also, to the memory of Olly, the irreplaceable German Shorthaired Pointer (2006-2018) my best friend for so many years.

Contents

Foreword

This book should never really have happened as I had no intention to write a novel of this genre at all. Indeed, in all of my life I had rather shunned the world of spies and their seemingly complicated lives of tangled webs and deception. I have never actually cared for James Bond ever since as a teenager I watched the first of the franchise films Dr. No. Too far-fetched and too reliant on gimmicks was my reaction then and indeed still is today. I did feel that the Bourne films were more exciting and had the seeming difference that the 'hero' did not seem guaranteed to survive!

After the previous publications of my poetry collections (Curses and Verses and Reflections) and my true-life story (Olly & Me) I was as far from thinking about creating this kind of frantic, fantasy thriller as I possibly could be.

No, I actually set out to write a deep, scholarly, profoundly moving expose of all that I had learned over the roller coaster journey of my three score years and ten. I intended it to be my final expression on life, death and everything in-between, my legacy, my closing statement, my swansong, my farewell to the world. Unfortunately, or maybe fortunately (or this book would never have been written!) when I set off staring at the proverbial blank piece of paper in front of me with absolutely no real conception of the story, the plot, the characters, my dreams of a novel to rival all the classic stories of the last hundred years was suddenly over before a single word had been written.

I had heard it said that sometimes the story just writes itself and in this instance that was literally true. It was as if my internal AI had suddenly kicked in and I was on auto-pilot for the first two thirds of the story just blindly typing away not knowing when the next character or situation would appear and where exactly this was taking me for at that point I was as ignorant as any first time reader as to the outcome of the very thing that was developing at a breakneck pace in front of my very eyes.

The urgency did abate somewhat over the final couple of chapters but even then, the plots and counter plots just kept pushing through my mind almost as fast as I could set them down in print.

So, friends, if I may call you that, here it is, not deep and meaningful, not scholarly and learned, not even revolutionary, no real depth of character profiling and perhaps not even a sustainable, believable storyline.

However, despite these obvious shortcomings, well if compared to my original lofty ideas, I believe that this is a fast paced, twisting plot format that I hope never gets turgid and boring and leaves you, the dear reader, with many unanswered hypotheses which might even provoke you to question the reality of what you once perceived as fact.

Who knows, but just maybe if the many ailments don't get me first and this book becomes even moderately successful, perhaps there will be (should be?) a sequel or three?

– Andy Casey
April 23rd 2025

The Power to lead is the power to mislead, and the power to mislead is the power to destroy.

– Thomas S. Monson

1
Setting the Trap

'Mr Owen, today is the 9th May, by the 23rd May you will be dead,' the voice said, that monotonous, deep, well-spoken voice with the clipped accent of indeterminate origin and the man of uncertain age and origin stared poker face at me. Apart from the near certainty that he was a white Caucasian there was no other possible clue to his provenance as he was almost totally engulfed by the shadows of the room lit by the solitary desk lamp that favoured my direction. He of the unblinking eyes and unwavering gaze stared straight at me through the gloom as if to study my reaction to this last statement. I gulped audibly and, not for the first time in this confrontation, my voice wavered as I stammered 'Dead? What do you mean dead? How? From what? I don't understand, I don't even know you. Is that a threat?' The man leaned back and his relaxed pose relaxed a few more degrees. 'No, Mr Owen, this is not a threat, it's merely a fact, a promise, a reality. You will be dead by the 24th May next, that is definite, it's only the place and manner of your death that are unknown but the act of dying is a certainty.'

I sat there frozen, you know that phrase, something about your blood running cold, well I knew now exactly what it meant, I was unable to assimilate exactly what this man was stating, I just couldn't absorb the full implications of his remarks and sat in silence trying desperately to get my brain back into gear. Suddenly, it was then that the complete absurdity of the situation hit me and like a flood of water bursting through a punctured dam, I started to laugh uncontrollably, my shoulders shaking with the intensity of my mirth. 'You are completely mad and I must be completely mad sitting here listening to such garbage, I don't even know you and you certainly don't know me and now after ten minutes of us meeting you're predicting my death? This whole thing is just too ridiculous for words and I am leaving now before I really lose my temper and do something I might regret later.'

'Sit down Mr Owen and listen very carefully.' The voice registered a very slight increase in menace, 'Let me recap the situation: you are Robert Owen of 19, Derwent Drive, London E7, you are 57 years of age. Your father is dead and your aged mother is in a care home, you have a younger brother called George living near you who is in the police force and you have an older sister living in Suffolk. You were a brilliant rising star in the army special ops unit, making a name for yourself in Northern Ireland, killed 6 IRA men by all accounts. You were very young and had a glittering career and then you blotted your copybook big time and had to resign or face a court martial so they say. After that you tried to emulate your little brother in the police force but again you were forced to resign, too much enthusiasm at policing those anti-war marches apparently. Then a retired Colonel from your old army unit helped set you up in business and with his finance and assistance you did in fact eventually take the firm into bankruptcy and he, poor chap, lost a lot of money, drink did for you this time so it's said. Now, you are, let's say resting, between jobs, you are divorced, no children and recently somehow acquired a new girlfriend called Claire who has no idea of your murky past or indeed of your occasional erectile disfunction let alone your drinking and your gambling habits. You are considerably in debt and have no means of paying back what you owe and the interest payments are rising every month. You are a third-rate author who wrote two very trashy novels and a volume of poetry, all self-published and all only bought by a handful of the very few friends you had and by some relations who probably felt sorry for you. You went from being a successful businessman with your own Company and all the trimmings - young sexy secretary, company car, expense account, pension pot and health insurance to a man who can barely afford to take his girlfriend to the local café. We also know that you have been diagnosed with terminal cancer and given a prognosis of two to three years of life without treatment and possibly up to five years with treatment and that you have a meeting scheduled for next month with the specialists when you have to give your decision. The only thing we don't know for sure is why you were so desperate for money, was it to leave something behind for your family? Was it to fund your bucket list? Or maybe it was to fund alternative treatments maybe abroad, in the States for instance? All things considered, Mr Owen, you are what most would describe as one of life's failures, until fate brought you here. You arrived here as a consequence of two things, your present situation and your greed for finance, is this not the case Mr Owen?'

'How do you know all that information?' Where did you find all that out? Who…'

'Mr Owen, oh may I call you Bob by the way, much more informal don't you think? Anyway, Bob, let me just say I know all that about you and far, far, more, I know what you eat, how you sleep, what you read, your favourite films, your go-to foods, I know your greatest fears and your wildest dreams. However, how I know is completely irrelevant and you are only muddying the already very murky waters by even troubling yourself as to how, you should really only be concentrating on the why.'

My false show of bravado and my even falser sense of humour had suddenly and completely deserted me as if this mystery man had thrown a bucketful of icy water over me. I recalled with more than a little sadness and distress how those texts had started to arrive, sporadically at first but then more frequently, then daily. Those stupid texts advising me that I had been randomly selected to take part in a brand-new general knowledge quiz, a quiz that promised instant cash prizes for every time I answered one of the general knowledge questions correctly. Not only that but the prizes seemed unreal, starting at twenty-five pounds for a correct answer and then doubling until the magic figure of one million pounds had been achieved. A simple game of comparatively simple questions to be answered in the five second slot allocated to each answer, the kind of easy challenge a Nags Head pub quiz winning team member could only dream of and the answer to all my problems, what could possibly go wrong?

At first it was that easy, at exactly 10.00am every day a question would be sent by text directly to my phone and, as easy as shelling peas, my answer, the correct answer, would be fired off within the allocated time slot. To put the icing on the cake the winnings would be in my bank account within an hour, no fuss, no quibble, this was the easiest money I had ever earned, God was thanked every single day for the bounteous gift that just kept on giving. Of course, once I had reached the one hundred and twenty-five thousand pounds answer it stopped being quite so simple and the winnings then went into an account that was not mine, but the promise was that it would be, even if I answered the last question incorrectly, I would still receive five hundred thousand pounds. To answer that final question in person is how I arrived at this modest semi-detached house in North East London and now stood quivering with fear and indignation as this man turned my excitement into fear and confusion.

'I still don't know what the hell this is all about, why such an elaborate scheme to snare a very unimportant ordinary member of the public? Tell me, what is this all about, why are you here and more to the point why am I here?'

Bob, you should not put yourself down; despite your many faults and your huge catalogue of failures you have a very unique skill that almost makes up for all the downsides to your character.'

'Really? and what the fuck is this skill?'

'It is the ability to kill Bob, very few can kill and even fewer can kill in cold blood like you have. Apparently, a couple of these IRA men you 'interrogated' took many hours to die.'

'That was different, that was war, it was kill or be killed I'm not a sadist, I didn't get any morbid satisfaction from my actions back then, I did what I had to do to stop our people being blown to bits, I am not proud of those times but you have to understand the context of these things, in war anything can happen.'

'Yes Bob, I agree with you entirely, but the fact remains that when push came to shove you could end another human being's life and not once but at least three times. That is a rare skill and Bobby it is why you are here today.'

'I don't know why some things that happened over 30 years ago have any bearing on today, the war with the bloody IRA has ended, haven't you heard of the Good Friday Agreement?'

'Yes Bob, that war is, to all intents and purposes, finished, but there are other wars, secret wars, not publicised, not a word in the papers or on the television, not ever officially mentioned in political circles but real wars nonetheless and Bob, unfortunately for you, your skills are needed more than ever to help fight that kind of war.'

'What bloody war? Is it against Russia, China, Iran? Who are we fighting? I say 'we' but I don't even know whose side you're on, are you MI6? In counter intelligence or are you fighting for the other side, whoever they are?

'Bob, there are some things which must remain a mystery to you and most certainly always will, it matters not whom you are fighting for or against, you are a mere pawn in one huge game of tactical chess and you will just have to be content knowing as little as that.'

I tried in vain to collect my thoughts but nothing he said made any sense, it was all a riddle in an enigma as someone famous once said, I tried to turn to my old subterfuge of bluff to see if I could understand the purpose of this nightmare. 'Now listen Mr - well I don't even know your name.' The man cut in even more abruptly.

'No Bob and you never will, no name, no pack drill as you army types like to say, again you are concentrating on the irrelevant subjects, rather than what should be your one question, how can I avoid a total catastrophe occurring in two weeks' time? All this other talk is just semantics, surely you want to know how you can survive not my name, rank and serial number?

'Ok Mr Mystery, I will play the game your way, what do you want of me and how can I live past the 29th May?'

'At last, we are finally getting somewhere. The answer to your question Bob is really simple - to avoid a premature and unpleasant termination of your existence you have to kill three people, that's all, just end the lives of three individuals using that skill you honed all those years ago.'

My blood, boiling at one point of this interview, now ran cold as for the umpteenth time in a very short period I tried to make sense of the words which my ears had heard but which my brain couldn't fully comprehend. 'You are bloody mad, in fact you're fucking insane, just kill three people, this sick joke has gone on quite long enough, I don't know why I have been sitting here listening to this drivel, killings and deadlines, threats and illogical scenarios, you are completely sick, I am leaving now and I am going straight to the police, you are at the least guilty of using threatening behaviour and at the same time very definitely in need of some form of therapy to sort out your obviously skewed mind.'

'Mr Owen,' the formal title now back in use. 'You can of course leave, you have always been free to go, I am after all not holding a gun to your head, at least not literally. However, even if you are stupid enough to go to the Police, you will find that you won't be able to tell them anything remotely criminal, in fact you will be wasting their time and indeed yours and time, Mr Owen, is something you are desperately short of. I am sure once you have had time to think that you will see sense and I will be waiting to hear from you, just text me on 3901 but again I would stress that every day you delay is one day closer to a very unpleasant ending.'

This last statement was said in the same calm, measured manner but this time the emphasis was a lot more chilling and made me feel distinctly less brave than the attitude I attempted to adopt. 'I'm going to the Police and then they will get to the bottom of this utter madness, goodbye Mr Mystery, I hope that I never see you again, unless it's across a courtroom.'

'Au revoir Mr Owen, but if I were you, I would think very carefully and don't delay.'

I rose from that chair, which felt like it had almost become part of me and without a backward glance headed for the front door as fast as my legs could carry me. On gaining the sanctuary of the public pavement I paused and at once broke into an enormous sweat, my heart pounding and experiencing sensations that I hadn't since those long-ago days in Northern Ireland. Finally catching my breath, I made my way to the nearest pub and, after downing a very large Scotch, I rang my brother George and trying to sound as calm as I could, asked if he could join me urgently for a drink.

Nothing is easier than self-deceit, for what every man wishes, that he also believes to be true.

– Demosthenes

2
Curiouser and Curiouser

George did arrive very promptly indeed: a very dapper man in his fashionable suit, thin tie and very shiny shoes, he was thinner than me, had more hair than me and according to most people looked a hell of a lot more than two years my junior or was it that I just looked so much older? Whereas I had been a rebel at school, a misnomer for a total failure, George had been diligent in all his studies and therefore, quite unlike me, he obtained the necessary qualifications for him to gain entry to university even if it was not considered one of the major ones. Yet again his application and sheer hard work led him on to further success and then, when it looked like he was on the verge of achieving his ambition of becoming a top criminal lawyer, it all came crashing down. He had met a girl at university, they had fallen in love and unfortunately, for his career prospects anyway, she had also fallen pregnant with the twins and the need to put a wage on the table resulted in George quitting University and enrolling in the police force. Once there he rose rapidly through the ranks, going from uniformed Constable to Sergeant then on to CID and the lofty position of Detective Chief Inspector in record breaking time.

In fact, you couldn't really get a greater contrast between two brothers. I played truant, frequently got disciplined for various misdemeanours, started smoking at the age of thirteen and drinking very soon after and was eventually shown the door at the age of sixteen with just a basic handful of 'O' levels and a very bad reputation. In the end it seemed like the army was the only organisation that would take a chance on me and I found that the life of a squaddie with its comradeship and travel really suited me far more than any boring desk job in civvy street would have. So, in our own way both brothers prospered in our forced positions, the only difference being that George carried on in an exemplary manner right up until the present day whereas I lurched from one disaster to another until I was eventually drummed out of the army suffering from acute anxiety and depression.

We had somehow remained close despite only having our parents in common. George not only prospered in his career but became a superb father to his four children and was soon in a position to afford them a private education and two foreign holidays a year in contrast to my failed, miserable marriage and twenty years of alcohol abuse and pill popping, mostly tranquilisers for my ongoing anxiety issues, but I was also not averse to trying any form of recreational drug that I could get my hands on.

Now here I was, desperate to receive some assurance and support from him in his official capacity and I felt like the younger brother sitting before him, his immaculately creased trousers, shining shoes and golf club tie reminders of the gap in our relative social status.

'Well Bob what's the matter this time? You sounded like this was very important and as you haven't contacted me for a social get together in many years you don't have to be a copper to deduce that you must need something, either advice, a shoulder to cry on or, much more likely, some money. I'm rather pushed for time as it happens, so be a good man even if you can't ever be a good brother and spit it out.'

'Well George, something happened to me today that is very strange, not to say frightening, I have been threatened with my life and asked to kill three people.'

'Hold it right there, is this a joke, a wind-up? Have you been overdoing the booze again, maybe adding something a little stronger? As I really haven't got time for this kind of fantasy talk, I'm back on duty in an hour and haven't had my dinner yet, so either get on with the real reasons I'm here or I'm leaving.'

That statement somehow got to me and all the pent-up emotion of the last couple of hours boiled over and, despite my best efforts to remain steadfast in front of my kid brother, I began to cry, gently at first then in uncontrollable waves of sobbing. George looked at me like I was some creature from the black lagoon, seemingly unable to comprehend that his older sibling was making such an exhibition of himself in public.

'Bob, come on, calm down, okay, you're not joking, I get that but you have to admit that it's still a very weird thing to encounter on a Thursday night in the Dukes Head?'

He was of course absolutely bloody right, maybe I could have phrased it better, so taking a deep breath, I proceeded to tell him the whole saga from the first apparently innocent text message to my encounter with Mr Mystery earlier that day. When I had finished, he looked at me very strangely and again wanted to know if I had been consuming alcohol in my usual copious quantities or had a wacky-baccy smoke or two or if I was suffering a relapse of my PTSD, to all of which I of course answered in the negative.

'Okay Bob, well let's start this from the beginning like a Police investigation,' his notebook was out by now and pen poised at the ready. 'These texts, you haven't deleted them, have you?'

'Of course not, they're the only proof of my winnings,' I said in my best hurt manner.

'Good, well let's have a look then.'

I scrolled through my recent messages, then I did so again and again but absolutely no trace, they had seemingly vanished into thin air. 'Listen George, they were all here not half hour ago, I actually was looking at them just before you came into the bar, on our mother's life, they were here, I swear.'

George gave an exaggerated shrug of his shoulders, 'Bob, you obviously must have deleted them without realising, if you let me have your phone tomorrow, I will give it to one of our boffins at the station, they can retrieve anything from any device so don't worry, they will get them back and then with a lot of luck we can trace the number. Now, even more importantly, these payments into your bank account, let's have a look at them.'

I opened my banking app and looked firstly at my current account balance, it stood at £227.66 but earlier today it was most definitely £125,227.66. I frantically scrolled backwards and forwards and even checked my savings account which, as usual these days, was empty. 'George, you may find this bloody difficult to believe but somehow those payments have been deleted and there aren't any transactions to see, I just don't understand what's going on, can people really hack into bank accounts and remove credit payments just like that and leave no trace that they have ever been there?'

'Oh, you'd be surprised what certain criminal organisations can do when push comes to shove but this is a highly sophisticated scam, it would appear that we are certainly not dealing with your average shoplifting gang. When I check the phone out tomorrow, I will also make enquiries with your bank to see if they can shed any light on this very peculiar sequence of events, the security at banks like your one is so tight these days there's a good chance these scammers have messed up. Now with the little time I have remaining I suggest that we pay a quick visit to this house you went to today just to check if there are any clues there.'

We duly exited the pub and made our way, walking at breakneck speed to Silcocks Road which was about fifteen minutes away. I confidently opened that metal gate, still creaking exactly as it had been earlier that day. Then I stopped, confused and hesitant. 'What's the matter Bob, this is the right place, isn't it?'

'Well,' I said.' I'm certain that this is it but I'm sure that it was no.19 earlier and the number on this door says 31, also I could have sworn that the front door was light blue and yet this one is brown?'

'Bloody hell Bob, are these people scammers, financial fraud experts or home decorating specialists? Are you absolutely 100% sure that this is the right house?

'Yes George 100%, look I even remember that tear in the curtain there, noticed it whilst I was waiting for Mr Mystery to open the door.'

George gave me another of his 'you are a complete moron' looks and then reached out and rang the bell; he waited a few seconds and rang the bell again only this time for much longer. Eventually and to my surprise, the door opened and there stood a middle-aged woman in her dressing gown peering up at us. 'Yes, how can I help you? If you're selling anything, we don't need anything, thank you all the same.' The woman stepped back and went to shut the door but George had already put one of his immaculately shiny shoes in the way and then from seemingly out of nowhere produced his warrant card. 'We are very sorry to disturb you Madam but we are here as part of an ongoing Police investigation and just have a couple of quick questions for you.'

'Police you say? Well, we're both law abiding citizens here, we haven't got anything to hide, so ask away.'

'Thank you, Madam, for your co-operation, now who actually lives here?'

'I live here, I have done for the last twenty-five years or so and my sister Rose also lives here, she's in the bath at the moment and we have 3 cats, we vote Conservative and watch wildlife documentaries on the television, is there anything else you'd like to know?'

‘Just two more things actually, you haven’t ever rented a room out to anyone? And have you and your sister been in the house all day?’

‘No, we have never rented, we couldn’t have strangers in our house, not with our cats and I have been here all day, Rose did pop out for a couple of hours to go to the local bingo, she’s bingo mad, can’t stand it myself, but takes all sorts I always say, is that it?’

‘Yes Madam, thank you for your help, we’ll be in touch should we require any further clarification, thank you again.’

George and I walked back towards the pub at a much slower pace, ‘George,’ I said, ‘either I have finally flipped my lid and I’m having lots of unexplained and crazy hallucinations or, well I don’t even know what else to say, even I find this all hard to believe now?’

George looked at me with what seemed like pity, put his hand on my shoulder which was a most un-George-like thing to do and mustering a half smile said ‘Listen Bob, the whole thing sounds completely diabolical to me and if you weren’t my brother I think I would be arresting you for wasting police time, then I would almost certainly be referring you for psychiatric evaluation. So, Bob, before I go and make a complete fool of myself can you for the last time confirm that all this really happened and that you have told me every single detail?’

‘George, as crazy as this sounds, every word is gospel, I promise you on our mother’s life.’

This last comment seemed to help with his state of mind and he visibly relaxed a bit. ‘Okay Bob, I’ll be in touch, I’ll get on to your bank tomorrow and you make sure you bring your phone into the station first thing and leave it at the front desk marked for my attention. I know this is easier said than done but don’t worry, things will be much clearer in the morning I promise you.’ With that last optimistic remark my dear little brother disappeared down the street at a very fast rate of knots.

Until you realize how easy it is for your mind to be manipulated, you remain the puppet of someone else's game.

– Evita Ochel

3
Things Heat Up

I actually walked back past the pub and for a change, kept walking until I reached the modest little ground floor flat which was now all that was left of my former wealth. I went in and pausing only for a much-needed shower, went to bed utterly exhausted by the events of this day that I would never forget for the rest of my life. My head hit the pillow and contrary to my usual practice I fell into a deep sleep, the like of which only usually occurs when myself and a certain Mr Jack Daniels get together in a big way. Then what seemed like just a couple of minutes later I was rudely awakened by the sound of my phone ringing as the bedside clock showed the ungodly time of 4.00am.

'Mr Owen,' said a familiar voice, a voice I thought I might never have heard again, 'how are you, did you have a nice brotherly get together with George tonight, I just can't imagine what you were discussing.'

'Now listen to me, I have told him everything, all about your threats and mad schemes and very soon there will be a knock at your door and half a dozen burly coppers will be standing there ready to arrest you.'

'Oh Mr Owen, that's not a very nice way to talk to the man who has your life in his hands. Anyway, Bob, what door will these stout officers of the law actually be knocking on? I am paying you the courtesy of this call just to remind you that another day has nearly gone and your time on this earth is slipping away fast, I urge you to reconsider your position and at least listen to my proposal. I am sure that once you fully realise the dire predicament you are in you will be a sensible fellow and co-operate. Think long and hard Bob and then contact me without any further delay.'

With this he rang off and left me laying there wide awake now with my mind racing and the end of any hope of a peaceful night completely shattered. I checked the origin of the call and all the screen showed was 'unknown number' another mystery call that I desperately hoped George and his boffins would be able to trace.

About an hour later, as I was tossing and turning, trying desperately to regain the deep sleep that had been so rudely interrupted a loud bang punctuated the early morning calm and at the same time a bright light illuminated my half open bedroom window. I instantly rushed to the window to see what looked like a sizeable fire in the car park of the flats. Bloody vandals! I thought to myself, if they're not stealing cars they're setting fire to them, should be bloody shot. Then in a flash I realised that I should be out there checking on my car and I hurriedly donned a pair of jeans and a jumper, jammed my feet into a pair of trainers and headed out to check the fire.

When I reached the car park my worst fears were realised, my blue BMW convertible, my pride and joy for the last fifteen years was a mass of crackling flames and billowing black smoke, the heat so intense that I couldn't get within twenty yards. As I stood there utterly mortified first one, then a second, then a third fire engine arrived and in a matter of what seemed like minutes they had extinguished the blaze and revealed a twisted metal wreck of what had once been a gleaming motor vehicle. Glass and other debris littered the road and some of the adjacent cars and there hung in the air an acrid smell of burning metal and petrol fumes.

I stood there trying to take in the scene and to make some sense of what I was seeing. A large group of people from the flats had by now arrived on the scene and were excitedly discussing the blaze as if it was some kind of firework display that had been enacted just for them. Just after that a police car arrived and they were immediately shown over to me by the nosey neighbours as the guy whose car had been burnt to a molten mess.

As there was absolutely nothing further to be done until the morning dawned the two police officers accompanied me back to my flat and proceeded to ask me the usual 'we have to ask these for the record' type of irrelevant questions that tend to annoy people who have just suffered the anguish of seeing their most treasured possession completely destroyed. They seemed satisfied that this was a case of pure vandalism and that I wasn't connected to any local drug gangs and they soon departed although they did leave me the all-important crime report number for my insurance company.

I decided that bed was now completely out of the question and went into the kitchen and made myself a coffee to which I hastily added a very large measure of Scotch, I was in dire need of something to stop the sudden shaking of my hands and that feeling of utter dejection which had started the moment I witnessed the aftermath of that horrible blaze.

After recovering my composure if not my nerve, I eventually showered and shaved, made myself some toast, butter and more very strong coffee for breakfast and then dead on the stroke of nine o'clock I rang the insurance company to make a claim, hoping that for a change they could expedite proceedings as I couldn't envisage my existence without my personal transport being always available.

After the frustrations of talking to a Bot for what seemed like an eternity, I finally persuaded her, him, it, to put me through to a human being in customer services where, after going through copious amounts of, in my view, completely unnecessary security questions, I told my story in as concise a manner as possible. After another long inordinate delay my not so friendly, in fact quite icy, almost hostile lady called June came back on the line.

'I am so sorry for your loss Mr Owen.'

'My loss?' Really, it was indeed said just like a funeral director would give you such concerned platitudes.

'But if you recall your policy was cancelled yesterday at 11.00 am and your refund for the portion of your cover not yet expired already paid into your bank account.'

I just stood there as in a trance for what seemed like a lifetime, then finally recovering my senses I forgot all normal forms of customer etiquette and almost screamed down the phone, 'I have not cancelled my policy with you, there must be some ghastly mistake, please can you check again?'

Another mind-numbing delay and this time the rendition of Greensleeves did not accompany it but just the deadly quiet sound of silence.

'Yes, Mr Owen I have a copy of the cancellation here. An email was received from you at 10.58 yesterday and our reply was acknowledged by you at 11.42.'

‘But I didn’t send any such email, in fact I didn’t send any emails at all yesterday, I was very busy doing other things.’

‘Mr Owen, is your email address bob.321owen@quickserve.co.uk?’

‘Yes, it is but I’m telling you, I didn’t send you any such email.’

‘Mr Owen, has anyone else got access to this email account?’

‘No, no-one, I’m the only one with access.’

‘Well then Mr Owen, I’m afraid that there is nothing we can do about it, if you wish to complain you should put your complaint in writing within the next thirty days to the address shown on our website. If you suspect someone has hacked into your email account, I suggest that you contact the police. Now is there is anything else I can do for you?’

‘No and thank you for nothing!’ I shouted and threw the phone down like a demented toddler.

Feeling completely drained by the events of the last twenty-four hours I sat back in my favourite armchair, poured myself a very large Scotch even though it was barely nine thirty in the morning and tried desperately to work out what the heck was going on in my life. In desperation I rang George and explained to him the latest disaster in my rapidly destructing existence. He listened, albeit in a slightly 'what's the matter this time' kind of manner which certainly didn't help my mood at all. Once again, he was blaming me, questioning my complete lack of responsibility and putting it down to my drinking habits.

I think I did finally convince him that this episode with my car coupled with the bogus communications with the insurance company was beyond my capacity to perform if stone cold sober, even less if I was inebriated as he was suggesting.

'Ok Bob, it does seem that someone is out to frighten you, to coerce you into carrying out this diabolical plan, someone with, it seems, infinite resources and access to all your personal information.'

'Yes Sherlock.' I said testily, 'I know all that but what I don't know is how the bloody hell I can make this all go away and I can get my life back.'

'Well Bob, I suggest that you bring your phone in now, I mean immediately and lets firstly see what secrets that reveals. In the meantime, I think you should take great care where you go, what you do and who you see as these jokers sound unhinged and seem capable of anything.'

'Well thank you for that very sage and comforting advice George, so now you think that they could actually do more to me than destroy my car?'

'Bob I'm not saying that your life is in danger, far from it, they obviously want you very much alive, just be careful, go into a phone shop today and pick yourself up a cheap phone and a sim only plan so that you have a means of contacting me and it will also get you a new number, just make sure that you don't give anyone but me that number, okay?'

I mouthed my agreement and set off for my nearest phone shop where for a small amount of money I purchased an old, basic smartphone, probably one of the originals by the look of it and that all important sim with a new number. Arriving at the police station I gave my usual phone to the desk clerk and asked that it be marked very urgent and passed immediately to Detective Inspector George Owen. That task accomplished I decided to retrace my steps and go back to my flat to see if any of my personal belongings could possibly be salvaged from my wreck of a car. Unfortunately for me, the police had excelled themselves and I found that the remnants of my car had already been transported back to their garage to enable specialist examination in order to determine the exact reasons for the blaze. All that remained were the scorch marks on the road and the heavy stench of flames mixed with water, foam and petrol along with my neighbour's car which had, in the cold light of day, suffered quite extensive damage. No doubt dear old Mr Greaves, the owner of that car would be knocking on my door very soon in order to get me to claim on my now non-existent insurance. He'll be lucky I thought grimly.

I wearily headed for my front door desperate for another drink and maybe even the solace of a few hours' sleep whilst I waited for the results of the police tests on the phone and car. When I got to the front door, I was puzzled to find that it was in fact wide open and therefore feeling more than a little apprehensive as I was certain that I had locked it earlier, I walked in and was immediately attacked by one, two, maybe three seemingly hooded figures who punched and kicked me until the sweet mercy of darkness came at last to my rescue.

It must have been several hours later as it was dark and I felt immense pain through every one inch of my body and also the cold sweat of fear and humiliation not to mention the severe cramp which also beset me from laying on that wooden floor. I gingerly, very gingerly, pulled myself up with the help of the nearest armchair and staggered into the bathroom whereupon I saw in the mirror that at least my face wasn't injured as I had still retained my rugged good looks My torso, neck, arms, legs and buttocks however, had, deliberately it seemed, taken the worst of the beating and were severely bruised and battered although taking everything into account I appeared extremely lucky that nothing, internal or external, at first glance appeared to have been broken.

I reached in the bathroom cabinet for some antiseptic spray and cotton wool and proceeded to dab the liquid all over the injuries, flinching and moaning with the pain that every movement incurred. Suddenly feeling extremely nauseous I was forced to stop my ministrations and instead I hobbled painfully to the toilet whereupon I was as sick as a whole pack of dogs, retching and heaving like it would never stop. Stop it eventually did and I finished my first aid duties and stumbling like a man in a gale force wind, almost fell back into the bedroom and onto the bed, dead to the world.

Later, much later when I finally stirred and managed to slowly, oh so slowly, drag myself out of bed and then literally crawl out of the bedroom to the solace of the lounge and then to the largest measure of Scotch I could fit into the glass I telephoned George and let him know of the attack. George of course was suitably shocked and advised me to call an ambulance as I possibly had internal bleeding and he would arrange for one of his men to meet me at the hospital to take a statement and photos of my injuries. I of course fortified by several large gulps of the Scotch refused this very sensible piece of advice and indeed would have put myself back to bed if George hadn't appeared a little while later and insisted on driving me to the local A and E department. Eventually, (why does an emergency department not act like anything is an emergency?) I was seen by a seemingly endless array of doctors and after undergoing a battery of various tests, scans and X-rays I was declared only bruised and beaten without any life-threatening injuries. They of course lectured me about my quite obvious high alcohol intake before finally allowing me to make my way, slowly and painfully back to George.

George took a full statement and one of his men then took more photos of my body than most Vogue models have in a year but eventually after much huffing and puffing the Doctors agreed that I could be discharged and George dropped me and a considerable number of different painkillers home but only after his man had firstly conducted a full-scale search of the flat, just in case, as George said.

I decided that trying to undress at this stage was quite out of the question and made myself as comfortable as I could on the sofa, grabbed a bottle of Scotch and the television remote and almost immediately fell into a deep sleep.

The incessant sound of my new telephone ringing brought my wonderful dreams of a sun-drenched beach and a sun-kissed dusky maiden to an abrupt halt. My God I thought, doesn't George ever sleep? However, it was not the sound of my brother's voice that greeted me but the rather more clipped, polished tones of my interrogator Mr Mystery. 'Hello there Mr Owen, I am so sorry for ringing you at this ungodly hour but as the phrase goes 'time and tide wait for no man' and in your case that is so literally true due to the fact that two full days have elapsed since our little chat and I'm sure that I don't have to stress to you again that your life cycle is running out fast now.'

'Listen, whoever you are, you've never even given me your bloody name.'

'Oh Mr Owen in the scheme of things that is hardly of importance but if you want to call me anything just use 3901, okay?'

'You want me to call you by a number – dear God what fucking planet are you on? In the last day I have had my car fire-bombed, been physically assaulted in my own home and now you are playing bloody secret squirrel games about your frigging name.'

'Mr Owen, calm yourself down, accidents happen you know and we all get these annoying days for no justifiable reason, just relax, we wouldn't want you to have a coronary now, would we? At least not until you have helped us in our little scheme.'

'Mr 3901 I think you are quite barmy, if you have really described the last twenty-four hours as just one of those annoying days then heaven help us all when we have a really bad day.'

'Quite dear boy, quite, anyway let's not waste any more of our valuable time speaking of your little mishaps, I need you to meet me tomorrow at eleven in the morning, I will ring you an hour before that time to give you the venue and Bob dear boy, I really suggest that you don't get the police involved. I think it will be much safer for everyone that way, so be a good chap and make sure you are alone.'

I went to reply and to tell him to stick his meeting where the sun doesn't shine when the line went dead and I was left in the dark in both senses of the phrase. Feeling extremely angry and in no mood to listen to the advice of the mystery man, I immediately rang George and put him in the picture 'Bob,' he said reassuringly, 'this is just what we want, I'd like you to come round to the station straight away and one of our men will fit you with a wire so that we can record everything,' he says. 'And don't worry, once you leave here to meet him we will be shadowing your every move and at the appropriate moment your Mr Mystery will be arrested and we can finally get to the bottom of what this bloody strange affair is all about.'

George actually swearing meant that he was deadly serious about this and was confident that we would have our man and his diabolical schemes under lock and key very soon.

Nothing more completely baffles one who is full of tricks and duplicity than straightforward and simple integrity in another.

– Charles Caleb

4
Down the Rabbit Hole

I left the flat in a hurry and had walked no more than two dozen paces down the road when all of a sudden, a large limousine with blacked-out windows screeched to a halt alongside me. The rear window opened and an all too familiar voice greeted me from the depths of the car interior 'Mr Owen, hop in please, we need to talk.' There was absolutely no way that I was going to step foot in that car but then the front window also opened and the unmistakeable sight of a gun barrel pointing straight at me suddenly induced a change of mind and I reluctantly entered the car, whereupon it sped off causing the still partially open rear door to slam shut behind me.

'Now Mr Owen isn't this pleasant? The two of us plus Jake the driver and Tony the, how can I put it, the minder, are going for a little drive to somewhere safe and private where we can talk freely without the need for wires, recordings or interfering police officers getting involved.' I sat there too dumfounded to offer even the slightest protest as the car headed out of the city and into the countryside.

We finally stopped in a semi-rural area where a large grassy clearing formed part of a car park overlooking a lake, this was obviously a favourite with picnickers as there were several wooden tables with bench chairs attached. Mr Mystery politely suggested that we should exit the car and have a seat at one of the tables.

So much for George's master plan, instead of entrapping Mr Mystery and having him arrested, I was now stuck with him and his two sidekicks, neither of whom would win any pleasant smiles competitions, in the middle of nowhere and at least one gun ready and waiting to be used should the right opportunity arise.

'Bob,' intoned Mr Mystery in that clipped but somehow laconic tone, 'there is absolutely no need for any further unpleasantness, I think that we have proved that we can have a very detrimental effect on your life and believe me, what has happened so far will seem like child's play if you don't become much more co-operative from now on. We have the ability to ruin your miserable little existence piece by piece or in one move and then there's your family, your dear old mother and your earnest but boring brother and his brood, now just one question Bob, are you going to be sensible, carry out this little job and receive a considerable cash payment or are you going to disappoint again?

The mention of my family and the possible harm to them had not crossed my mind and certainly added a whole new dimension to the situation and put me in a completely new and quite undesirable dilemma. 'Listen, there is absolutely no need to bring my family into this, they are completely innocent of any wrongdoing, especially when compared to my somewhat chequered past and harming them would not in any way achieve your objective, I can assure you. I don't like mysteries, never have, never will and I just don't understand why you or anyone else come to that, should go to all this trouble for me. Surely there are contract killers, assassins or whatever term you use to describe them that could carry out these killings for you at a fraction of the cost, time and effort that you appear to have already wasted on me?'

'Mr Owen.' he said, switching back to the formal 'There are indeed professional killers, assassins if you prefer but believe me the good ones are very few and far between and therefore highly sought after, also they are regrettably very well known in the circles that count. Furthermore, sometimes, as in this instance, a complete unknown is required, someone who has no track record, has not been crisscrossing the world on assassination missions and is to all extents and purposes an insignificant man. Unfortunately for you Mr Owen if this quality is combined with your proven cold-blooded capacity for killing that makes you the perfect person for our plans.'

'You are of course right in your assumption that we have not stage managed all you have encountered over the last few days, it would not only be expensive and dangerous but impractical and time consuming.'

'So, what are you saying? These things didn't happen, I made them up, imagined them?'

'Actually Bob, you are not too far from the truth, you have heard of AI, Artificial Intelligence? Well, there has been a further advance on that called AAI, Advanced Artificial Intelligence that is capable of performing such amazing tricks that most people wouldn't think are possible. Do you remember recently in the pub meeting a man called Jerry Summers?'

Jerry Summers, yes, I remembered him, a loud, red-faced giant of a man with a very loud transatlantic accent, I remember his opening line when he accidentally bumped into me in the pub, thereby spilling my drink and being so apologetic. 'So sorry sport, never did look where I was going, manners of a mountain goat so my Lorraine says and I guess she's right, let me buy you a refill, I insist, least I can do.'

He did indeed buy me a drink despite my protestations that there was no need, I was on my way home but to no avail and so soon we were sitting down with a couple of pints and very large whisky chasers in front of us on the corner table he had directed me to.

'Well pardon my manners, my name is Jeremy, Jeremy Summers but everyone and I mean everyone knows me as Jerry and you are?'

'Pleased to meet you Jerry, my name is Bob, Bob Owen and many thanks for the drinks.'

Then we sat and chatted, he told me all about his home in Oregon, showed me photos of his wife and kids and explained that he was a fine wine salesman, though he gave it some other high-faulting title but that's essentially what it boiled down to, selling large consignments of quality wines to hotel groups across Europe.

It appeared that we had the love of American football in common and by an amazing coincidence it turned out that he too was a great fan of the Dolphins, my all-time favourite team. He proved a very interesting and entertaining, if a little loud and overbearing, companion and although I didn't keep count, I know that we were downing drinks like there was no tomorrow. In fact, I don't recall exactly how, where and when we parted so it must have been a very heavy session indeed.

'How the hell did you know that I met Jerry?' I demanded, don't tell me he is also part of your crazy little plan?'

'Mr Owen, it really doesn't matter how I know or what I know, suffice it to say that out mutual friend Mr

Summers had a major part in preparing the ground for subsequent events.'

'You mean it was a setup? He didn't accidentally bump into me and knock my bloody drink over?'

'No, not exactly but again Mr Owen let's not get bogged down in what he did or didn't do, the point is that he played a part, a part he has played many times before with great distinction, I might add.'

'If you mean by that he is good at lying and deception I will agree with you, and I suppose he's a bloody bomb expert too and was the one who blew my fucking car up?'

'Mr Owen, you still don't get it, no-one blew your car up, no-one assaulted you and your brother has absolutely no idea that you are in this predicament.'

'So, you're saying that I have been seeing things, things that don't exist, making all this up, that these things never really happened? I don't bloody believe you; I heard the car get blown up, I saw it burning, I felt the bloody kicks and punches, I've got the bruises to prove it.'

With that I lifted my shirt and displayed the welter of black and blue contusions that covered my arms, abdomen and chest and displayed them to him.

'Who the hell do you think did this?' I shouted in exasperation and more than a hint of triumph.

'Bob. That night you met your new best friend Jerry and after consuming way too much of the hard stuff, you had a fall, a bad fall down those concrete steps that lead from the pub. You obviously don't remember but you were in a right state, the Paramedics spent ages cleaning you up and tending to your wounds. You really should have gone to hospital like they suggested. I suppose that old soldier stiff upper-lip attitude came into play then eh Bob? Listen there are lots of things that are not what they seem. If you don't believe me, use your phone and ring your copper brother and ask him about the last couple of days, be my guest.'

I didn't hesitate to take up his offer and rang the number in a state of something approaching euphoria, perhaps now I could stuff his fine words right where they rightfully belong.

'Hello George?'

'Hello Bob, how are you? Bit of a surprise hearing from you. Thought you'd done another one of your disappearing tricks, how's things?'

I could feel my face flushing with red hot rage. 'George,' I shouted, 'is this a wind-up? What about the assault, my burnt-out car, what the hell is going on?'

‘Calm down old boy, I haven’t a clue what you are on about, have you been on the sauce again, remember what Dad always said that it would be the ruin of you?’

‘George,’ I practically screamed down the phone, ‘just be very honest with me, when did you last see me?’

‘Well let’s see, must have been a couple of months ago when I lent you that money for your car service, not that I’m mentioning that because I want it back, all in good time, no rush, I trust you.’

I was more shaken than I had been ever before in my life, even the events of the last few days palled before this sudden shock to my already highly stressed system, I muttered a few pleasantries and ended the call, what the hell was happening to me?

‘So, Bob, how’s our George? I should think he had a surprise hearing from you and all that stuff and nonsense about assaults and fires, he must think that you are finally cracking up.’

‘Listen, Mr M or Mr Y or Mr fucking 999, whatever you call yourself today, I know that you have somehow arranged this whole bloody thing.’

‘What, I have bribed a police officer, and your brother to boot? Surely Bob you must now realise that all this nonsense is just a symptom of your overactive imagination.’ His voice suddenly changed from the calm bantering almost jovial tone to that of ice-cold precision.

‘Mr Owen, the time has come to end these timewasting little games of yours, you have now seen our capabilities, you know that we are deadly serious and now we require a straight answer from you, are you prepared to carry out this assignment for us or not?

I looked into his unblinking eyes but the previous friendliness had vanished and I saw absolutely no sign of any humanity and goodwill in his determined expression. I knew the fate of myself and my family were at stake and I therefore took the only possible decision I could.

‘Okay, you win, I will do what you want, as long as you guarantee no harm will befall myself or my family?’

‘of course, Bob, you have my word and may I congratulate you on finally making the right choice, I am a very non-confrontational man and I am genuinely pleased that you have seen the light and decided to become part of our little adventure.’

‘So, what happens now? When do I find out exactly what my part in this is going to be?’

‘Don’t worry Bob, it actually starts immediately, let me introduce you to my colleague who will be accompanying you on this venture and will fill you in on any details, well only the ones that you need to know of course’

With that he waved his hand at the second car which must have arrived without me being aware and out of the back seat a figure emerged, a female, an apparently very young female, tall, slim and easy on the eye.

'Bob,' he said as this woman approached us, 'this is Nadine, at least that is what you will know her as, she will be your mentor, your guide and your confidant in this matter, do not be fooled by her looks, this lady could kill you stone-dead before you know it, in fact she is under orders to do just that should you fail us at any time. So, Bob, make sure you follow her instructions or you won't even be making the end of the month and I will be truly sorry if that were to happen.'

He got up and strode away, got into the rear of car and sped away down the road, perhaps leaving my life altogether and good bloody riddance after the mayhem he had caused in it over the last few days.

Meanwhile Nadine, about my height, a modest five feet eight inches when standing fully upright, dressed all in leather, short jacket and leggings which displayed a great pair of legs and a very pert bottom and other womanly curves too, had arrived in front of me and immediately extended her hand but not for me to shake, no this babe obviously wanted the whole works and somewhat reluctantly I pressed my lips to her hand.

We are nothing but lies, duplicity,
contradictions and we hide and
disguise ourselves from ourselves.

– Blaise Pascal

5
Nadine

'Hello Owen.' she said in a decisive authoritative mid Atlantic voice that contained maybe just the slightest detectable hint of an eastern European background sometime in her distant past, I put her as about thirty-five years old but there again I am rubbish at guessing ages so she could well be ten years either way. She was attractive rather than beautiful, maybe her mouth just a tad too large and her nose again just short of perfection but with her figure, long glossy dark brown hair, any shortfalls in appearance were absolutely minimal.

'Hello Nadine.' I said back as strongly as I could muster, not wanting to show any sign of weakness at this stage of our relationship. 'Perhaps you can explain to me what the hell is going on and maybe you would also care to call me Bob as it looks like we are going to be on the same side at least for a while?'

'Owen is just fine,' she shot back with no hint of friendliness in her voice.' We are here to do a job, you are only here to follow my orders and to know just as much as you need to know, which is very little indeed, do you understand?'

'Look Nadine I have been assaulted, kidnapped, probably drugged, brainwashed, whatever you may call it and now I'm with a stranger with whom I am about to go and kill unknown bloody people in unknown bloody places for unknown bloody reasons and you expect me to be calm and carry on regardless?'

'It appears that you already know exactly as much as you should do in your position, believe me it is better for everyone, including you, that you are not aware of the full details of what is planned and why. I too only know slightly more than you, knowledge as they say is power and the less knowledge you and even I have the better in the scheme of things. Just trust me, do as you're told and you may well get your life back, start causing problems and asking too many damn questions will only lead to one outcome and I hope that I don't need to spell that out?'

'Okay, I won't ask any more questions for now but I can't promise that for the future, this crazy adventure and all you crazy people in it makes the mad hatters tea party look quite normal and I still would like more information before I even contemplate killing anyone'

'Owen let's stop going round in circles, either you are coming with me or you are staying. So, make up your mind as we have an aeroplane waiting for us that is due to take off in three hours' time and if you are not on it there will be severe consequences, so make your decision now.'

With that she turned on her heel and walked swiftly back towards the waiting car leaving my mind in yet another turmoil. A plane waiting for us, so almost certainly abroad, so my so-called contingency plan to play for time and to get word to George of my latest predicament was already in tatters. Taking the safest option, I duly followed her figure down the hill and got into the front passenger seat through the already opened door, noting that she was ensconced in the rear, no doubt reminding me of my subordinate place in the team.

The car sped away and we drove for at least an hour until we arrived at a small commercial airfield in Hertfordshire. One twin engine Learjet was the only plane on the tarmac and its engines were already chugging impatiently as we raced over the grass perimeter towards it.

Upon entering the plane Nadine spoke in a whisper to the pilot and withing a few minutes we were airborne and heading into the unknown through a rapidly darkening sky. 'Can I at least know where we are going?' I asked as soon as the need for seat belts was over. 'Yes of course Owen, we are on our way to Austria.'

'Austria? Really? Any chance of actually knowing why?

'Because, as should be fairly obvious to anyone with half a brain, our quarry is there.'

'There? Where exactly is there?'

'Owen you won't believe this I know but we are both heading into the mountains to find solace and peace of mind in a monastery, probably the closest you've been to a house of religion since you attended Sunday school at your local church as a small boy, many years ago.'

A monastery? Even I was dumfounded by this answer, I had expected an expensive villa even a royal palace, assuming that our intended victim was a highfaluting politician or royal of some kind or even a Mafia boss but it had never crossed my mind that they would want me to kill a complete stranger in a house of God.

'Don't worry Owen, all will be revealed as we get further into our little adventure, in the meantime, put these on as where we are going is a hell of a lot colder than where we have just flown from.' With that she handed me an all-in-one ski suit, a thick woollen bobble hat and a pair of sturdy boots complete with a pair of thermal socks. 'These should fit you; they know your sizes and in this holdall you will find more changes of clothes, underwear and personal toiletries, don't forget to take it with you when we disembark.'

I hastily donned the proffered outfit and checked the contents of the holdall, as Nadine had said, it contained a couple of changes of clothes, toothbrush, razor, deodorant and everything else a man needed to keep reasonably clean and well groomed. It surprised me in the sense that it was either my own toiletries presumably taken from my bathroom at home or someone had gone to the trouble of purchasing the exact brand I always used. Despite everything I couldn't fail to be impressed with their thoroughness, whoever they are.

Within what seemed like a fairly short time, a time unpunctuated by any talk between us, the pilot announced that he was making his final approach and it was time to put on our seat belts and to prepare ourselves for landing.

When our plane touched down without the merest hint of a bump, God I wished I could fly like that, I at first wondered if they had played one more trick on me and we had landed back at the same airfield as we had left a few hours before but it proved to be a different if similar small country style aerodrome made very ghostly by the almost complete absence of lights.

Waiting patiently at the side of the landing strip was a large robust looking four by four with the engines running and after stowing our holdalls in the cavernous boot we got into the vehicle. Nadine this time took the front seat next to the driver with whom she engaged in animated conversation for some time in a foreign language completely alien to me. As the journey continued through the night the road got narrower and bumpier and the weather deteriorated from light rain to heavy snow with a corresponding dip in the temperature. I was glad of the change of clothes even if growing more apprehensive of what was awaiting me at journeys end as each mile was completed.

Eventually, after our vehicle took a notably higher altitude route, we finally came to a halt at a service area of sorts, not so much Toddington Services more like Bram Stoker's isolated community stopover. We exited the car here and Nadine informed me that our destination was now just another forty-five minutes further up the mountain and that it was time to discuss the plan of action for when we arrived there.

'Now listen carefully to this Owen, your life, indeed both our lives, could ultimately depend on your ability to comprehend and obey these instructions. Firstly, the common languages spoken here are Italian and German, you of course have no great knowledge of these languages but be very careful as most of the inhabitants on the monastery have more than an understanding of English. Secondly, there is no talking or indeed eating allowed between the hours of seven am and six pm, everyone rises from bed at around six am for breakfast so I suggest that you eat as much as you can then for there is a long time until you eat again. We are officially known here as father and daughter, we have adjoining rooms, well when I say rooms they are apparently little more than cells formerly occupied by monks and they are no doubt very basic and uncomfortable. There is a shower room and toilet down the corridor from our rooms and not one door in the entire building is locked or indeed even has a lock. We are here for the peace and tranquillity, to pray, meditate and grow closer to God, at least that's the official reason and let me tell you that for very basic accommodation, very scant food and absolutely no luxuries of any kind, they charge visitors like us an awful lot of money. I will identify our target and then we shall put the next part of our plan into action, you shall be told what that actually is as you soon as you need to know. Now, any questions?'

'Any questions? I have hundreds; supposing we are asked where we live, how we live, about my supposed wife, your supposed mother, our line of work, our past histories together and more, much more?'

'Owen, you worry too much, no-one suspects we are here for any other reason than to bathe our souls in God's reflection and spend time in solitude, peace and calmness in a place of holy consecrated grounds which is permutated by the complete absence of the violence, unease and frantic pace of the outside world. However, just in case, in order to cover every eventuality, they have prepared some basic information on our current and past relationships, read this dossier, memorise it then tear it to pieces and flush it down the toilet here before we leave. You have twenty minutes, so get reading as I shall be testing you on the remainder of our journey.'

I settled down to read the through the proffered documents which were the size of a small novel, it seemed this lot were definitely prepared for every eventuality. Nadine meanwhile had managed to find us a spare table in the rather over-brightly lit refreshments room, I refuse to call it a restaurant due to its clear lack of hygiene and obviously non-existent health and safety rules. Our fellow travellers were either trailer drivers or local farmers I assumed and they all appeared to devour the mediocre food with considerable relish. My stew was lukewarm and consisted of a very thin watery broth complete with some root vegetables and some very tough meat of unknown but certainly dubious origin. The generous portion of bread was almost stale too although the coffee was strong, hot and flavoursome.

We then went back into the weather that had turned from feeling chilly to being downright freezing, our feet crunching and slipping on the icy pathway leading back to the car. True to her word, Nadine did quiz me on the dossier for the remainder of the trip and though I didn't actually receive any spoken praise, her grunts of approval convinced me that I had passed that particular test with flying colours.

Soon, all too soon for me, we stopped at a large metal gated entrance with a tarnished and well-worn sign bearing the legend Certosa di Sudtirol with an engraving of a kneeling monk seemingly crying to heaven in supplication beneath a giant cross although part of this was obscured by years of wear, bad weather and bird droppings. 'This is it,' Nadine said. 'This is as far as the car can go, we walk the rest of the way up the hill, get your holdall and be careful as the path will be lethal underfoot.'

We both retrieved the holdalls from the boot and after bidding farewell to the driver to include another bout of animated whispering between him and Nadine, we made our way through the unlocked gate and trudged warily up the steep path towards the large group of buildings that loomed ominously and theatrically out of the driving snow. Upon reaching what appeared to be the main entrance to the largest building we entered into an uncovered courtyard area with several doors leading off and without breaking stride, Nadine guided me towards one of these, pushed the door open and we were suddenly out of the near blizzard and into the comparative warmth of a dimly lit entrance hall. A cowled figure suddenly appeared out of nowhere causing even Nadine to register surprise by means of a startled intake of breath. This monk, I guess middle-aged with a sallow complexion and extremely tall and lean smiled at us, revealing a mouth of brown stained broken teeth. 'Welcome to God's house of Sudtirol, the Abbot is expecting you, please follow me,' He whispered in heavily accented English and led us to yet another door but one of far superior quality, mahogany or similar with brass fittings and a little brass plate with an effigy of Christ on the cross placed in the middle of the door.

'The Abbot is very hard of hearing,' he said to no-one in particular. 'You will have to speak up,' he warned and it struck me as funny that in this place of quietness and peace with him speaking in a very reverential tone we were being asked to shout at the half deaf head honcho. After a brief and almost casual knock on the door he pushed it open and ushered us in. The room was plain, very plain with whitewashed walls which were adorned with portraits from various biblical scenes and lit poorly only by a single light. The Abbot, who was not wearing a cowl, was completely bald, short and again very lean, I guessed he must be well into his eighties, rose from the plain and rather austere, basic looking desk, and held out his hand first to Nadine who bowed over it and brushed her lips against the knuckles and then to me who, breaking all protocol, grasped it firmly and gave it a hearty English handshake.

'Mr Owen and Nadine, you are both very welcome to this house of God, may your short stay bring you both peace and tranquillity and enable you to get closer to our Lord God so that when you return home you may experience the wonder of his earthly kingdom in ways more uplifting that you ever have before. We will talk again in more detail but I am sure that you must be very tired after your long journey, so unless you have any immediate questions, I will ask Father Bellucci to show you to your quarters and to explain the rules of this monastery for guests such as yourselves.'

'Thank you, Father Ricci, I'm sure that my dad and I will gain much from this stay and we look forward to talking to you over the next few days, I know for certain that my dad is very anxious to improve his knowledge of all things religious and is really very excited to be in such a place as this.' I stood open-mouthed at the effrontery of this statement but playing my part as a caring, dutiful parent nodded enthusiastically whilst wishing that the earth would swallow me up.

We took our leave and followed the thin, very thin cowled monk out of the room and down a long barely lit corridor, me following behind as he went through the various dos and don'ts with Nadine, obviously taking her as the more intelligent, responsible person and relegating me to a far lesser role in the long walk down the corridor which seemed to stretch for ever.

When we arrived at our designated quarters, I could see that basic was a very apt description if not over generous in that each room, if that term could be justified, situated on opposite sides of the corridor consisted of an area barely more than three metres long by two metres wide furnished with a thin mattress covering a raised stone ledge. On the whitewashed walls each room had an oil painting of some luminary from biblical times, a few clothes hooks and three small shelves for clothes. No sign of a wide screen television or a luxury ensuite anywhere. I was tending to be of the opinion that I was glad our stay was not intended to be a long one as even by my modest home standards this was certainly erring on the sparse side of sparse.

Father Bellucci then took us almost to the end of the corridor where he pointed out the shower and toilet blocks, the male ones consisting of a communal shower area, four WC's and four wash basins. It must be chaos on the mornings when upwards of thirty monks and guests are trying to make use of the facilities at the same time I mused. The female block was even smaller, consisting of a single shower, one WC and a wash basin, it was however slightly more luxurious with more fancy tiles and decent flooring, making me think that this must have once upon a time been the Abbot's personal bathroom now sacrificed for the sake of outside guests and for the precious revenue that they brought.

Returning to our rooms we were left by the good Father with a reminder to get some much-needed rest as the night was nearly done and the bell for morning prayers would be ringing in just a couple of hours' time. As soon as my door was closed and forgoing any niceties of washing, cleaning teeth etc. I lay down on that uncomfortable bed and despite my original misgivings I immediately fell into the deepest sleep that I could ever remember having, perhaps the best since my last posting in Northern Ireland had finished all those years ago.

The bell when it did wake me from my slumbers was far, far too early for my liking and I was definitely inclined to forget all about breakfast and to spend the day in bed but a loud knock on the door was immediately followed by the entry of Nadine who looked at me with something approaching disapproval and sharply ordered me to get to the shower room as we had no time to waste laying around on my fanny in bed as she charmingly put it.

I did indeed jump to it, perhaps I hadn't quite forgotten my military training after all, making my way to the shower room whereby I had to keep reminding myself that talking was still forbidden and that the best I could do was to offer a fixed smile to the several mostly ancient Fathers who were also indulging in their morning ablutions. The atmosphere was decidedly tepid, much like the temperature of the shower and once again I felt for the poor buggers who actually paid a lot of money for this extremely dubious privilege.

After a much needed all over wash, a shave and brushing my teeth I did indeed feel refreshed and once again like a human being as I joined Nadine, who had been waiting diplomatically outside the shower room, and made our way to back down the corridor to the central dining hall where we were warmly greeted by Father Bellucci who had waiting for us at the entrance and seems to have been appointed our personal guardian for the tenure of our stay.

Firstly, everyone stood in a very orderly queue in of course complete silence and then were served a bowl of steaming porridge oats from a vast and ancient looking vat, this was the only breakfast on offer but you could add to your porridge by helping yourself to some dried fruits and nuts from two separate large bowls placed besides the vat. There were also hunks of coarse brown bread on a huge wooden platter but no butter or spread of any kind. The only hot beverage on offer was a very strong black coffee which you poured yourself from one of several silver pots although there was no milk or cream to weaken the taste. Large jugs of water and earthenware cups were already present on the dining table and this completed the repast on offer. Having availed ourselves of these delicacies we were shown to our allocated places near the far end of the table by Father Bellucci, sitting together but with a monk on either side of us.

At precisely seven am the Abbot rose from his seat at the head of the table and spoke for a few minutes in a foreign tongue, Italian presumably and immediately he had finished speaking the bell rang once again and the hitherto total silence was immediately broken by the babble of thirty voices all seeming to want to talk at once. I took the opportunity to look along the large rectangular table to really study for the first time the inhabitants of this establishment. From what I could make out and that wasn't easy seeing that it appeared that cowls had to be worn at all times, the overwhelming majority of the monks were at least sixty plus years of age, mostly all thin and of sallow complexion which rather belied the image of men from this part of the world who generally appeared swarthy and of a healthier appearance.

The one exception to the rule was the monk sitting immediately to my right who by contrast to the others was more like a baby in comparison, I would have guessed his age at around thirty and noted he was tall, seemed of muscular build and had a nice even tanned face that peered out smiling from behind the obligatory cowl.

'I'm Father Philips, pleased to meet you,' he said in a most definitely Cockney drawl, are you and your wife staying here long?' Thanking him for the unintended compliment I corrected him that Nadine was in fact my daughter and our stay was to be of very short duration as the monastery was just one of a series of retreats that we had planned for the coming months. I spun him the previously agreed yarn that I was actively considering retirement to a place of God where in peace and tranquillity I could see out the remainder of my days in a land far from the cold, damp climate of England. This seemed to resonate with him and he opened up about his own spiritual and physical journey to arrive at this place at this time. He was a member of this order of very recent vintage having only been inducted a couple of months earlier. He had apparently led a typical middle stroke upper class life of women, wine and song with the emphasis most definitely on the wine. On a mostly drunken journey across Italy, he claims to have suddenly been confronted by God and in his own words 'once I saw the face of our Lord and heard his words, I had to follow him and pledge to spend the rest of my life praising him.'

Nadine, who had been listening to this dialogue without comment and with apparently only polite interest, suddenly took part in the conversation and skilfully managed to get him to spill the gossip on his fellow monks, their characters and peculiarities, leading him further down the road of confession whilst fixing him with that warm, beautiful smile of hers. It was obvious to me that nothing much that Father Philips had so far said really sparked her interest although he couldn't have possibly guessed that from the attentive gaze and encouraging murmurs of alternatively approval, disbelief and friendliness she gave him.

It was only when he dropped his voice almost to a whisper and told us his tale of a certain Father Ernst Hoffman that I sensed her marked change of attitude and almost excited anticipation though she was doing her best to control her feelings and to gently probe further for the good Father to reveal more than perhaps he should have done. It appears that Father Hoffman had appeared out of the blue approximately two months ago and the assembled brethren were informed by the Abbot that he was a repentant sinner suffering from a terminal illness and had taken the vows of the Monastery as he wanted to spend the short time he had left on earth amongst men of God. He was not though taking part in any communal activities but instead spending his days in splendid solitude, praying for forgiveness and redemption for the grievous sins he had previously committed. Our Father Philips was however sceptical about this story, declaring that he didn't believe that this man was even a monk at all: once he had apparently spied him through the half open door to his cell minus his cowl and this was not Father Hoffman's only sin, it was also obvious that he did not have the shaven head that all the monks of the order had. In short, Father Philips espoused, he was a fraud and also very creepy, staying in a room on the first floor as remote from everyone else as he could be, eating his meals in solitude and on the rare occasion that he was seen by any of the other fathers, not only keeping his distance but walking around with a superior bearing far removed from the demeanour of a repentant sinner.

The most compelling and indeed most worrying thing that Father Philips told us was that this mystery monk also appeared to have a bodyguard, a huge cowled figure who apparently shadowed him throughout the day. This was indeed interesting news for anyone who for instance had designs on killing the said Father Hoffman. Perhaps it could even be my salvation as what had seemed like a simple assassination, if such a thing exists, would now be far more difficult, maybe even impossible?

Later that morning back in my room Nadine soon corrected that forlorn hope. 'This man, whom you now know is called Hoffman, is our target and must be killed no matter what and even if he does have a bodyguard that will make things harder, it cannot and will not derail this operation. In fact, I have just a few minutes ago received word from outside that the assignment (how different and sanitised that sounds compared to murder) must be completed tomorrow without fail.'

'Tomorrow? Now listen Nadine that is far too soon, you said that we would have at least a week possibly longer in order to properly work out a plan for this thing to take place efficiently with the least possible risk to you and I. Now despite learning that this man is protected twenty-four seven, maybe even by someone with a firearm for all we know, they suddenly want us to rush in, kill him and get out with just a day's notice. I have to tell you even at this late-stage Nadine that I honestly don't think I could do it, to kill a stranger on the orders of God knows who for no apparent reason in cold blood, it's not who I am anymore, this is just plain murder and I am not inclined to have any part in it no matter what the consequences are.'

Nadine stared at me, her face more intent and serious than I had ever seen before 'Now listen to me, you may have suddenly got cold feet but this innocent couldn't hurt a fly routine doesn't cut any mustard with me. You have killed men before, maybe often as you say in cold blood but even worse you killed them with calculated coldness, you tortured and, in some cases extended their pain and suffering just to gain some information. You had no remorse then as you didn't stop after the first one, I think six were actually killed by you or on your direct orders, so spare me the crocodile tears please.'

'Nadine, I agree that I did terrible things, things that I am now utterly ashamed of but that was a different time and they were completely different circumstances, it was war, these people were maiming and killing not only my fellow soldiers but also innocent civilians, mothers, babies, aunts and uncles, they had to be stopped at all costs and they all knew the risks involved. It was kill or be killed, some of the guys from my unit suffered horrendous torture followed by very slow and painful deaths too. That was not peacetime Italy in a house of God slaughtering some poor bastard for what to all intents and purposes is no good reason at all.'

So, Owen, it was war and that justifies everything you did? Don't you understand that this is war too? Oh, it might not be uniforms and tanks and men with fancy titles saluting each other and getting medals for their heroic deeds. No, this is war of a different kind, where vastly powerful forces wage combat in a different manner, more covert than overt but just as deadly. Don't you understand that whilst mankind exists there will always be struggles for power and it is the poor innocent bastards caught in the crossfire that suffer. In whose name did you really maim and kill those men? And those men, those brave warriors of the IRA, who sent them to bomb and murder? On whose behalf were they really carrying out atrocities? Let me tell you, if you didn't already know, that your war was masterminded by a small group of politicians in London and by a small group of fanatical men in Northern Ireland calling themselves patriots. Neither side were really interested in justice and peace, neither were willing to give way and to talk until it was far too late and thousands had been maimed or killed. Owen, this is the same tawdry game, the identical craving for power, just carried out in the most part far more privately but just as deadly. These men, including the ones who have sent us here don't listen to reason, don't care about human decency, are impervious to the rule of law, they still play the game by the rules of the jungle even if most of the time they are using financial muscle assisted by cyber intelligence to achieve their wicked aims rather than the Kalashnikov and the bomb.'

Her face and voice softened as if the effort and the passion of her words had suddenly drained her. 'Bob,' the use of my first name was at once reassuring as it was also disarming, 'you must be aware of two things, firstly, I am in the same position as you, my family too are at risk, my mother, father and my two sisters could all suffer if I refuse to carry out these orders. Secondly, this man Hoffman is no innocent old priest, he was in fact quite a senior officer in the Stasi, the East German security force. Just like you he did some terrible things to people but unlike the men in your care, the people he tortured and killed were not hard-bitten terrorists but innocent people whose only crime was to put up a poster, daub some graffiti or try to escape to the West. He was evil personified and his victims numbered hundreds over the years he was active, by all normal standards he should have been put on trial for crimes against humanity and instead of taking in the fresh mountain air as he is doing now, he should be in prison and be kept there until he dies. He only survived until now because of friends in high places, because he could afford to bribe his way out of any charges, because the Government didn't want any scandal, preferred to sweep the terrors under the carpet in case it raised a reminder of the Nazis and the persecution of the Hitler years. No, he is going to die tomorrow Bob, and you and I are going to save ourselves and our families and also right a terrible wrong by killing him.'

I sat there stunned, all the fight in me and the clever arguments I had rehearsed over the last couple of days had suddenly vanished and I was genuinely moved by the emotion displayed by Nadine.

'Nadine, ok I get it, your family is at risk and our friend Hoffman is an evil bastard who probably deserves to die and I will do it but I am still far from happy about taking the life of what is now a harmless old man who may have now genuinely repented all his many sins and doesn't deserve this kind of unlawful justice.'

Nadine looked at me and then, very unexpectedly, stood up and held me close, I could smell the sweetness of her perfume and fell the wetness of her tears as they continued falling in an unabated flow.

'Bob, both you and I know that it's not right, not how it should be but we really don't have a choice, it is genuinely a matter of kill or be killed and not only us but our innocent relatives too. Now I have suddenly very limited time to try to ascertain the movements of Hoffman and the best time and place to carry out the action.' Action, again not using the word murder. 'By the way you haven't yet asked but the method of killing will be painless for him even if that is far more consideration than he ever gave his victims. We will go over the details before tomorrow's deadline, in the meantime just keep your eyes and ears open for anything that might help.'

With that, she turned on her heel and walked out of the room leaving me alone with my thoughts which was not helping my sanity one little bit. Oh, for a bottle or two of brandy I thought, hopefully more than enough to completely blot this unfolding ghastly scenario completely out of my mind. I suddenly wished for the humdrum existence I had left in London in what seemed like a different life, a different age.

It seemed far longer but within a couple of hours Nadine was back and back in her usual efficient, concise and businesslike manner, all trace of her earlier weakness and vulnerability completely gone. 'Bob, I have been doing a bit of ferreting, mostly with our loud-mouthed chatterbox Father Philips, it appears that Hoffman says his prayers at exactly seven pm every night without fail, no-one else present, not even his bodyguard. These devotions usually take around one hour, so in that time, we must strike and it has to be tonight as Father Philips has heard a rumour that he will be leaving the monastery very soon.'

'Tonight? My God that soon and how?'

Nadine extracted a small velvet box from her bag and opened it to reveal a sort of small, hypodermic syringe sitting on a crushed velvet cushion. 'Bob, this little beauty contains a drug so lethal that with any contact on the skin the victim will die without fail within a couple of seconds, you don't have to even find an artery or a muscle, just jab it through the cowl at the base of the neck and our man is a gonner. You don't need to push the plunger just literally ensure that the tip of the needle touches the skin and be even more careful that it doesn't touch your skin as there is no antidote, no treatment, you will die without exception This drug leaves absolutely no trace, completely undetectable by even the most modern medical techniques, it causes an immediate and fatal heart attack and as this man already has a history of heart disease, there will be no reason for anyone to suspect foul play. If you keep your nerve and proceed with the ice-cold precision you were chosen for, it will be a formality and this time tomorrow, we will be on our way home without any suspicion of any kind being placed upon us.'

'Nadine, you do make it sound very easy and so straightforward, but this is a human being we are killing in cold blood in surroundings we have never seen before and by a method I'm not exactly skilled in, I do want to believe you but something tells me that the old saying what may go wrong, can go wrong is still very relevant.'

'I am aware that there could be difficulties Bob but maybe, just maybe this is the time when everything goes completely smoothly and that is what we both have to believe and with the right amount of luck it will happen, just trust me. We will meet back here at six pm and discuss the plan and go over the main points again, I'd better take that syringe back, we don't want any accidents between now and then, not when we are so close and Bob, don't worry, it's all going to be fine.' Then she shocked me for the second time that day by giving me a warm hug and gently brushed her lips against mine before she left me alone once more.

I spent the rest of that day trying hard, without success, to put thoughts of the coming evening out of my mind, my body cried out for the comfort of an alcoholic drink or two but instead I spent miserable hours alternatively giving myself rousing peptalks about my abilities to overcome any obstacle and then convincing myself that I was no longer cut out to be a killer.

I had endured so many doubts and misgivings about this whole crazy caper. I felt suddenly nervous, vulnerable and very lonely as Nadine and Father Philips were nowhere to be seen. I made my way back to my room where I attempted to recall the meditation I had practiced religiously day after day to ease the tensions of my duties in Northern Ireland. Unfortunately, it didn't have the same calming effect, partly no doubt due to the absence of alcohol which we all consumed, indeed over-consumed, in those days to prepare us for the harrowing duties that awaited us.

Late in the afternoon Nadine suddenly appeared and was again all businesslike and very serious. She told me that she had gleaned two further pieces of information, firstly that the latest weather reports had confirmed the imminent arrival of a long and ferocious snow storm that would apparently cut the monastery off from civilisation for at least a few days, maybe up to a week. All roads would become completely impassable and we would be trapped here for the duration. This information only reinforced Nadine's desire to get this mission accomplished at the earliest possible opportunity and to get out whilst we still could. The other priceless nugget she had unearthed concerned Hoffman's routine, which apparently had never varied once since his arrival. Apart from his hour-long prayer session at the same time every evening he was also in the habit of having a small flagon of red wine delivered to his door at precisely eight pm. This duty had fallen to our friend Father Philips but Nadine had somehow managed to convince him that we would relieve him of this particular job that evening, apparently assuring him that the Abbot, thankfully absent for the day, had given his personal approval to the plan.

Whilst I was still digesting the information that some lucky bugger was getting served alcohol at this self-proclaimed dry establishment, Nadine was instructing me on how we would place the syringe next to the flagon on the tray under a napkin, thus almost eliminating the possibility of me accidentally coming into direct contact with that lethal drug and also making it far easier for me to pull back the napkin and plunge the syringe through the cowl into the back of his neck.

We spent the next couple of hours going over the strategy and timing until I could have carried out the assignment blindfolded, my confidence grew and like Nadine I began to see this as a very straightforward piece of action as long as Hoffman kept to his usual routine and I kept my nerve.

Just before seven pm Father Philips arrived with the tray bearing the flagon of wine and as soon as he had left, Nadine carefully removed the syringe from its case and placed it under the napkin which she had procured from somewhere. We waited another fifteen minutes to ensure that our target would be well into his devotions and then we exited the room and made our way along the corridor, me in front bearing the tray and Nadine a couple of paces behind me making sure no one else was following us.

We ascended the steep wooden staircase, my legs trembling with the tension and then I gently pushed open the single oak door where by the dim light of a few candles I saw the kneeling figure of Hoffman and heard his almost whispered chanted incantations of devotion. Moving as swiftly as I dared and as silently as I could I went to remove the napkin but as I did so another door at the rear of the room suddenly opened. I dropped the tray with an almighty clang and the kneeling figure turned round only to reveal the startled face of Father Ricci, the Abbot staring up at me with complete bewilderment. At the same moment several muffled gunshots rang out in the room and turning round I was confronted by the sight of Nadine with the still smoking Luger pistol in hand standing there with a horrified expression on her face. Turning back, I saw three bloodstained bodies lying in various positions in the room. One body was of the aforementioned Father Ricci, a bullet into the back of his neck, the next was through the chest of the supposed bodyguard who had obviously been in closer attendance than we had thought and last but not least was the body of Hoffman, another head shot; upon checking I found all three as cleanly killed as one could ever see.

'Bob, I had no choice, I didn't know this was going to happen, this shouldn't have bloody happened, why oh why was the Abbot here and where in hell did he come from?' she said in an almost hysterical voice pointing towards the prone figure of the bodyguard and in the next instance she dropped the gun and started to cry, the tension and sheer terror of what had just occurred causing her usual self-control to splinter into a thousand pieces. I went up to her and held her in my arms and allowed her to cling to me as she sobbed uncontrollably. 'Listen Nadine it wasn't your fault, no one could have known that this was going to happen, I'm bloody sure that you saved my life though because without your intervention I'm certain that the bodyguard would have killed me, he was ready to fire, look his gun is still in his hand.' It was only at this very moment that I became aware of a feeling of wetness running down my arm and was startled by the sight of a large red patch just above my elbow which was pouring out copious amounts of blood, my blood, in a seemingly never-ending stream. At the same time the pain also registered with my brain and I suddenly felt weak and sick to the pit of my stomach.

'My God, Bob you're hit, let me have a look at that.' Tears forgotten in an instant as the ice cool Nadine was suddenly back in control. She ripped the arm of my shirt up past the elbow and moving me towards the light of one of the candles thoroughly examined my wound. 'Bob, you are a very lucky man, the bullet has just entered the fleshy part of your upper arm and exited without seemingly touching the bone. Let's get you back to my room where I have a small first-aid kit which should, fingers crossed, be all we need to patch you up.' To be very honest at that moment I didn't feel very lucky, I just wanted a very large brandy and then about a month in bed until all this hideous dream had played itself out and I could return to normality again.

'But what about these?' I gestured to the bodies lying on the floor. 'We can't just leave them here, like this'

'Bob, what can we possibly do with them? We can't simply drag them along the corridor and out through the main entrance, this is the best place for them. There is absolutely no reason for anyone to come looking for them, all the monks have dispersed to their quarters, the Abbot wasn't due back until very late tonight according to Father Philips so with any luck they won't be missed or discovered until the morning which gives us several hours to get clear of here. So let's make the most of that time and get going.'

I was about to argue but something told me that I was beating my so tired head against the wall so I said nothing but followed her out of the room just about remembering to retrieve that bloody syringe before I did so. When we got down to her room without cause for any further alarms I began to relax, in fact I began to have a feeling of euphoria as the pent-up emotion and tension of the last half hour was suddenly released. Nadine for her part got on with the job of cleaning and bandaging my arm which was still bleeding but now only a trickle compared to earlier.

‘Bob I will contact our Masters now as arranged and tell them that the mission has been successfully completed, they will send someone to pick us up within the next couple of hours so I suggest that in the meantime you try, hard as it may seem, to get some rest as we have a long journey in front of us. I will have to think about exactly what we are going to do once they have dropped us off at the safe place. You do realise Bob that once this disaster is known we will be fugitives, we will have a substantial price on our heads and they will want us dead as soon as they can arrange it.’

‘Dead? We have carried out their fucking stupid orders, we have killed their man, okay I admit that it didn’t go completely to plan but the end result is the same, surely that will count in our favour.?

Nadine made a grimace, ‘Bob, you don’t understand, these people aren’t just worried about the end result and anyway this isn’t the end result that they desired, they wanted our friend Hoffman dead from a routine, non-suspicious heart attack, what they didn’t want is for him to be laying in a pool of blood with a bullet in him let alone two further blood-spattered bodies lying beside him. To them this is a complete and utter failure, we have failed them and they have to ensure that we pay with our lives for what they will consider an operational catastrophe.’

With this bone chilling statement Nadine left the room and suddenly the exhilarating feeling of a few minutes ago had completely disappeared, I gingerly made my way to the toilet and was as sick as I have ever been in my life. I cleaned myself up and returned to that bloody uncomfortable bed in an effort to get some sleep, hopefully a deep sleep that would stop my mind racing and calm these negative, frightening thoughts that had now invaded the inner sanctities of my mind.

When Nadine returned a while later, I was still wide awake, indeed I had found it impossible to relax in any way as images of the bullet wounds and the blood on the floor interspersed with that confused look on the face of the Abbot and the sight of Nadine standing there with the gun just would not leave my mind.

'How are you feeling now Bob?' Nadine said, her usual tone now back. 'I'm feeling fucking sick to my stomach Nadine, I thought I had seen enough bloodshed during my time in Ireland not to be affected but I was wrong, completely wrong. I feel that my life has turned into a bloody nightmare and it's getting scarier by the minute. I didn't want to have any part of this mad-capped scheme to start with and I wish now that I had tried to run when I had the chance, a bullet in the back and a quick death would have been preferable to this unholy mess we are now in.'

'Look Bob, I can understand your feelings, I feel devastated that two innocent people have been killed by me and a third, even if he deserved his fate, is also dead and we are in the deepest shit we could be in. But we are where we are and sitting around feeling sorry for ourselves is not going to change a thing. I have contacted the organisation and given the codeword that means the mission has been successfully completed. With the imminent arrival of this storm, we may well have several days before the news gets out about this fiasco and we must make use of that time to try to get as far away from here as possible. They will be collecting us within the hour and if we beat the storm we can be in the designated safe house before daybreak and at least gain some breathing space to decide our next moves. What you have to remember is not to give any hint to the driver that we have in any way messed up this operation, as far as he and they are concerned it all went exactly to plan, you got that Bob?'

'Yes Nadine, I've got that and I will go along with it because I haven't really got any other choice although part of me doesn't now really give a fuck and I am half tempted to stay here and take my chances with the local police.'

'Bob, when they come it won't be the local police, it will be them and believe me they will make what you did in Ireland look like a kid's tea party when they get hold of you, you won't just be executed, they will want to make an example of you for your perceived failure and that will not be a pleasant experience. So, forget any heroic thoughts about staying here and facing any kind of legal justice, get your things together and be ready to leave, quietly and without fuss as soon as I get the call.'

I did as I was told and packed my belongings back into the holdall and was ready if not too willing when Nadine came to me an hour or so later and told me that they were waiting for us outside. We made our way through the deserted corridor and gently coaxed the massive iron security bolts free to enable the main doors to open. Outside the weather had really turned for the worse, the night sky made even darker by what amounted to a near blizzard and several inches of snow had already built up underfoot as we gingerly made our way back down the track to where the waiting car stood, its lights almost obscured by the thick blanket of falling snow.

It is only prudent never to place complete confidence in that by which we have even once been deceived.

– Rene Descartes

6
Run For Our Lives

When we arrived at the waiting four by four Nadine got into the front passenger seat next to the driver and as soon as we pulled away was engaged in a quite animated but whispered discussion with him which seemed to end in a very amicable fashion with them both laughing seemingly at some unexplained joke. I for my part settled down in the large warm space of the rear seats watching the snow continue to fall like a solid white sheet of virgin white cotton wall, so dense that one couldn't pick out any individual snowflakes. I also marvelled at the skill of our driver who navigated his way along the narrow, treacherous track that passed for a road as nonchalantly as one out for a Sunday morning drive in the leafy roads of Surrey, one hand casually gripping the wheel whilst the other made flamboyant gestures to a smiling Nadine.

After a while and despite my best efforts, I finally gave in to the feelings of utter exhaustion and when I finally awoke some while later found that we were now enjoying much better weather and indeed much better roads and indeed the sun was timidly peeking through the clouds announcing the dawn of a new day. Nadine and the driver were still engaged in their whispered conversation although as it was entirely conducted in a foreign language of which I knew not one word, they may as well have been using loud hailers for all the difference it made to me.

Several more hours passed and we were then thankfully allowed a comfort break and the chance to get a coffee and a sandwich at a small bar/restaurant that seemed to be the local equivalent of a motorway service area. From the ongoing hub of conversation and the signs that hung around every wall I gathered that we were now in France and somehow that fact made me feel better even though I had never had any particular love for our friends across the channel.

We continued our journey for another few miles and then turning off the main highway we took a small dirt track surrounded by high evergreen hedges and eventually arrived at a small white farmhouse complete with rustic barn. Here Nadine and I exited the vehicle, collected our holdalls and were greeted by a smiling and seemingly very friendly young couple who wished us a very good morning in the most perfect English. Once inside they introduced themselves as Ian and Jan recently emigrated from the wilds of Norfolk to start a new life in the lush fields of Northern France. Of our mission or indeed our reasons for being there, not a word was uttered and we were obviously very keen that this continued so that our lies could be kept to an absolute minimum.

After a hearty brunch of eggs, ham, crusty bread and some rich crumbly home-produced cheese washed down by a coffee for Nadine and a large glass of Claret for me they showed us to a large comfortable bedroom with a large king-size bed and a clean and practical ensuite. They told us to freshen-up, rest and relax until the evening when they would prepare us a cooked meal and brief us on the local amenities that we could enjoy over the next week that we were scheduled to stay there.

Laying on the bed I almost dropped straight off to sleep again but was rapidly dissuaded from this course of action by Nadine who in a subdued voice explained to me her concerns about the wiseness of us staying there for one more day let alone the designated seven. 'Bob, we may have several days before the news of the deaths at the monastery reach the outside world but I don't think we should take that chance and therefore I think we should wait until dark tonight and then, using the car that they have put at our disposal, head straight for Paris.'

'Paris Nadine? Why Paris, why not head for the channel and see if we can get on a ferry or hire a boat whilst we are still in front of them?'

‘Paris Bob because that is where our next victim is and it is the very last place that they would expect us to head for. If word has got out about the monastery killings the ports and train stations are the first places they will be waiting for us.’

‘Hold on, are you mad? Surely after what has happened, you’re not going to go through with another killing? Haven’t you had enough of that because I have, I never want to see another dead body again especially an innocent one covered in blood.’

‘No Bob, of course we’re not going to carry out the killing but only by tracking down and talking to the intended victim have we got any chance at all of making sense as to why all this is actually happening.’

‘So, we are going to stroll up to Mr or Mrs whatstheirnames and say that we were going to kill you but having made a terrible mess of our last assignment we thought you might like to have a friendly little chat to us and tell us why you think you were going to be our next victim?’

‘Well yes, that’s about the drift of it though maybe we could approach them in a bit more circumspect way and anyway what alternative do we have? We can’t just go on the run and hope that your lovely copper of a brother will protect us, aren’t you at all curious who these jokers really are and why they want these people dead?’

'Well, if you put it like that then of course I am as keen as you to know why our families are in danger and just why we are trekking around the continent bumping off aged monks who appear to be just harmless old men waiting to die in a house of God and certainly don't seem to be dangerous in any manner. So, Paris it is and let's pray to God that they aren't even more clever than we think and haven't already double-guessed that we are stupid enough to hang around giving them even more chance of killing us'

Having showered, separately, we both then relaxed on the bed, side by side if not actually entwined like lovers at least close enough for there to be an obvious physical connection and without a care for any possible repercussions we were soon tearing each other's few remaining clothes off and indulging in lovemaking in what can only be described as intimate, powerful and at the same time terrifying in its intensity. Nadine, as in every other aspect of her character, was a determined and passionate lover, overwhelming me with her animal-like frenzied assault on my body and my senses. Indeed, her all-consuming and reckless attitude to love-making left me at once highly satisfied and then also briefly worried that maybe she thought that there may not be many more times to enjoy the pleasures of the flesh. Afterwards, we did lay as lovers, in complete silence, each savouring this brief moment of pleasurable sanity in an otherwise crazy interlude of our lives. Indeed, so relaxed were we that we both drifted off to sleep and it apparently took several attempts of loud knocking on the door until we awoke and found Janine summoning us down to dinner.

We got through a nutritious but more than slightly surreal dinner with every diner just using small talk to break the embarrassing silences, they once again didn't ask us any probing questions about our mission and we in turn didn't press them into divulging how exactly they had been recruited into this strange but deadly organisation. As soon as we had finished eating, we went quickly back to our room where we sat together all ready to depart on the stroke of midnight. I decided that I needed to make use of the few hours left by catching up on my sleep and feeling not only tired but for the first time in days quite relaxed, was soon deep in dreamland.

I was rudely awakened by Nadine shaking me and telling me that I had to get up that instant and look out the window. At first, I could see nothing but following Nadine's whispered instructions I finally made out the shape of two cars parked about a mile from the house in a place on the track where it widened to let vehicles pass each other. Their lights were dimmed and there appeared to be at least three, maybe four shadowy figures standing together in the dim light, they all looked ominously big.

'Bob, it must be them, no-one drives down a lane like this at ten o'clock at night, they must have found out about what happened at the monastery and if they have, I don't think they will be here to award us any medals for our actions. We must get out now but not down the stairs, Ian and Jan are still up and remember it could be them that alerted our friends outside. We must get out the back window from the landing onto the outhouse roof and then to the barn and the car. Don't bother about the holdalls, I have passports and money so we can worry about clothes and any other stuff later, for now we need to travel at our lightest.

Leaving the holdalls under the bed covers which gave an impression, at first glance anyway, of two people sleeping there, we quietly opened the bedroom door, made our way across the landing and then just as quietly opened the large side hinged picture window. Nadine went first, dropping down onto the tiled roof of the outbuilding and then clambering down the drainpipe until she reached the ground. I followed at a much more sedate place, believing the old adage more haste, less speed and slowly edged my way out of the window and onto the roof, dislodging a tile on the process and then holding my breath as it fell to the ground with what seemed to me like a terrific noise. I looked at the house but nothing appeared to change, no movement or lights, just the flickering of the television through the half-opened blinds of the front lounge. Thanking God for some luck as last, I managed with some difficulty, lots of effort and even more swearing, to descend down the drainpipe to join Nadine, who had been viewing my progress with not a little anxiety.

We entered the barn and Nadine told me to wait by the doors so they could be opened at the most opportune time then she got into the driver's seat of the ancient Citroen car, started the engine first time and then we waited in complete silence and bated breath in the darkness of the dilapidated building. After about ten minutes we saw the shapes of four men appear out of the gloom and make for the house, 'As soon as they go in, open the doors of the barn.' Nadine whispered through the open car window.

The men stood outside the front door for a few minutes talking to Jan and Ian and then they all entered and the front door was closed behind them. I immediately pulled open the rickety wooden gates as swiftly as I could and then got into the car as Nadine slowly eased the car out of the barn and past the house. She drove at the same unhurried, careful pace until we got to where the two cars were parked on the passing place of the lane. Here she stopped and got out of the car and then from point blank range fired a bullet into both front tyres of each vehicle. I meanwhile was looking out of the rear window of the car and suddenly saw the farmhouse front door open and two or three figures emerge. I then heard the sound of one or maybe more guns being fired which I somehow guessed were in our direction and called out to Nadine 'Will you get back into the bloody car and let's get out of here before we're shot to bits.' Nadine didn't need a second invitation and getting back behind the wheel accelerated with all the power the old car could muster down the remainder of the lane and finally onto the well-lit main road - we'd done it!

After driving at top speed for twenty minutes or so Nadine pulled into a layby and said to me 'how are you old man?' Not quite liking the name tag I replied 'Just fine, there's nothing I like better than escaping from an upstairs window then clambering down a roof and finally being shot at by vicious thugs.' She laughed and surprisingly drew me close to her and put her lips to mine, a long passionate kiss followed and then she said 'Well it's not really my idea of fun and not what I signed up for when these missions were put to me but apart from your little scratch you got at the monastery we're unharmed and now have a good head start on those guys back there who hopefully, when they get new tyres will be on their way to the channel ports whilst we head to Paris.

'Anyway.' she continued, 'we now have several hours of travelling to endure and this old thing has never heard of sat nav so I need you to stay awake and help me navigate. How about you tell me your life story, that certainly sounds like it will inhibit any thoughts of sleeping.'

'No, Nadine, you will find my life very boring and besides you have already been briefed a fair bit about the highs and mostly lows of my existence. However, I don't know anything about you and I am very keen to learn, especially finding out how you came to be a crack-shot with that pistol of yours.'

'Okay Bob, that's fair enough, I suppose you do deserve to find out with whom you are driving about Europe putting your life at risk. I was born in a little town just outside Bucharest called Ploiesti. I would like to say that it is charming, picturesque, beautiful even but I 'm afraid like most Rumanian towns in that area it is a grey, industrialised, uniform collection of tower blocks and drab small shops. I went to school there but at the first opportunity I headed out to Bucharest to go to university. I was one of five children, and yes, you've guessed it, the middle one with two brothers and two sisters and regretfully none of my siblings made it out of there like I did. I suppose I was just lucky in that I had from somewhere inherited a natural talent for learning languages and by the time I left University I was fluent in English, French, Italian and Russian with a fair knowledge of German and Hungarian too.'

'After completing my university course, I was conscripted into the army for a year, it was still compulsory then, and I found myself seconded to a sharpshooting regiment. After twelve months of intensive training, I left the army as an ace in terms of rifle shooting but strangely enough my pistol shooting only warranted an average score. Therefore, all in all we were lucky that at the monastery those men were very close to me and I couldn't really miss or we would not be enjoying this trip today.

After leaving the army I was at a complete loss as to where my future lay and then due to my foreign language skills I was approached by the Rumanian secret service and after several lengthy and in-depth interviews I began work for them. Mostly, especially at first, it was extremely boring, transcribing documents, translating tapped telephone calls and the like, not the glamorous existence I imagined it would be. I did finally get to do a few field trips, sitting in on trade meetings as a translator and sitting in bars listening to drunken Russian diplomats telling state secrets to cheap whores.

It was on one of these field trips to Rome that I was approached by your friend Mr Mystery offering me a new career in working for the organisation. I was offered an extremely lucrative salary and all the perks for duties in translating which seemed quite easy and interesting, certainly more interesting than working for the Rumanians. However, it didn't take me long to suss out that they weren't exactly a bona-fide concern and I tried to resign but then the threats to my family came and I reluctantly agreed to oversee these three missions in return for a large financial reward and, more importantly, my freedom. So, here I am now, driving across France in fear of my life being pursued by nameless thugs intent on doing me harm after having killed three complete strangers for no real reason. To add to my misfortune, I'm in the company of a washed-up ex-killer, current drunk and terrible assassin, a middle-aged Englishman with a paunch and a terrible history.'

'Nadine,' I said. 'You really do say the sweetest things about me but I have to take issue with at least one of them, I am not a drunk, at least not now, on this trip from hell I have barely consumed the amount of alcohol I would normally quaff at my local pub in one short session. I'm actually quite proud of myself for this abstinence as I have had multiple excellent reasons for hitting the bottle big time in recent days.'

'Oh Bob, if only I could believe that given the chance you would not have drunk yourself absolutely legless at every God given opportunity but I don't think that our present situation leads itself to wasting any more time arguing about the validity of your drinking habits, good or bad. Let's just concentrate on getting to Paris and finding this man, who by the way is named Albert Klein and who is, in polite circles anyway, a quite well-known concert pianist. We are going to front him up at his luxury hotel on the outskirts of Paris where he is resting before performing next week for the French President.

Of course, if the original plan was still in operation, he wouldn't be performing any more concerts for anyone ever again as he would have been dead by next Thursday. However, due to this favourable turn of fortune, favourable for him anyway, he will still be able to entertain the glamorous Parisian nobility at the swanky Elysee Palace.'

'Nadine, this man Klein, another German I assume? What has he got to do with anything? Now I'm far from a lover of classical music but why would anyone want a concert pianist murdered? What's the connection between him and our poor dead wannabe monk Hoffman?

'I have not got the faintest idea Bob, they only told me the whom, not the why I'm afraid, perhaps there's no connection at all, perhaps we're just going round Europe killing people to satisfy someone's sick sense of humour or maybe the maestro Mr Klein played one too many wrong notes and upset on of our anonymous leaders. We will hopefully soon find out but in the meantime, I suggest that you make yourself more presentable at the next service area we come to, a wash and shave will help and maybe some deodorant and aftershave too? This is a very exclusive and exorbitantly expensive five star plus hotel we are heading for and I want my husband to look as respectable as he possibly can.'

'Husband? Well at least that's an upgrade on being your father, and are we going to be ensconced in the honeymoon suite my darling wife?'

'Don't push your luck Bob, I'm warming to you but there's no certainty of a repeat performance of what happened in the farmhouse. However, if you play your assigned part to absolute perfection, with impeccable manners and a distinct lack of admiration for the nearest sherry decanter, you never know what might occur over the next couple of days.'

With that we pulled up outside the service area and having eaten a substantial meal we ventured into the small provincial town where the shops had just opened and bought all the required toiletries to make us feel more like human beings again. We then went to a very old-fashioned menswear shop and bought me a cheap but passable suit, shirt, tie, socks and shoes whilst Nadine went to a more fashionable chic boutique outlet and purchased a rather lovely and obviously classy two-piece ensemble complete with matching shoes and bag. We made our way back to the service area and spent time in the washrooms making ourselves as presentable as we possibly could.

When we eventually arrived at the hotel, I could see what Nadine meant about it being a classy affair. It stood proudly perched on top of a hill, a magnificent old chateau looking centuries old with an impressive tree lined drive way leading to a large ornate courtyard where as you stopped your car myriads of flunkeys swooped to assist even before the engine had been turned off.

We booked in under the very quaint and quite original names of Mr and Mrs Smith and were escorted to a lavish suite with a balcony and breathtaking views over the palatial gardens and large picturesque lake. Our bed was enormous and very comfortable but all thoughts of passionate lovemaking or even blissful sleep were immediately dispelled by Nadine who announced that we should confront Mr Klein at the earliest possible opportunity and then, if all went well, there could be plenty of time to try out the bed later.

Going back down to Reception we asked one of the many staff that hovered everywhere if they could confirm the whereabouts of a certain Mr Albert Klein as we were from the English press and had an exclusive interview with him. After being told that that they couldn't possibly give out any confidential guest information, they had a sudden change of mind when Nadine slipped quite a large wad of Euro notes into their hand. 'Mr Klein is on the Lakeview Terrace taking afternoon tea,' we were informed and after receiving directions we set off to find our former quarry who had now been elevated to maybe our only hope of salvation. Nadine and I had discussed beforehand how best to approach Klein and I was all for the honest bluff approach which instantly met with a withering look and the comment 'Bob, are you out of your tiny little mind? You think that the best way to introduce ourselves to him is to say, we just killed three men and were sent here to kill you but we have now changed our mind and instead would like some information.' I must admit that put like that it did seem a rather dumb way to approach a very delicate matter but at least it got us to the core of the matter without the need for going round the houses and without further delay.

In the event we eventually agreed to play the conversation 'by ear' and just to see how it developed, after all the three of us did have one common purpose in this murky affair and that was staying alive. So full of false optimism coupled with a nervous excitement and great anticipation we duly made our way to the splendour of the Lake Terrace where we were directed to the table on the substantial outside balcony overlooking the lake where our Mr Klein sat.

Albert Klein was an impressive figure, elegant, tall and wiry with a mop of white hair and a similar coloured goatee beard which added a look of further gravitas to the overall impression and belied the age of seventy-two that Nadine's dossier had bestowed upon him. His long-tapered fingers were holding a bone-China cup and he appeared to be enjoying the Earl Grey tea which he poured himself from the matching teapot.

'Mr Klein, Mr Albert Klein?' Nadine asked

'Yes, that is me and to whom have I the honour of addressing?' Mr Klein had a strong deep voice which almost contrasted with his somewhat slight looks but his English was impeccable with barely a trace of a foreign accent

'My name is Nadine Smith and this is my husband Bob, we are both admirers of your work and when we heard that you happened to be staying in the same hotel, I'm afraid we couldn't help but try to seek you out.'

'I am very pleased to meet you Mrs Smith and you too Mr Smith, now is there anything in particular you wish to know?'

At this stage I forgot all the rehearsals and Nadine's strict instructions and, leaning forward I asked in a soft voice 'Mr Klein do you know a man called Mr Ernst Hoffman?' I sensed Nadine tense and saw the surprise and anger in her face but I was determined to have this out in the open without further delay.

'Ernst? Yes of course I do, I have known him for over half a century. He is one of my dearest friends, why do you ask? How do you know him?'

'Well, Mr Klein it's a very long story and I'm afraid that we have break the bad news to you that your friend Mr Hoffman is dead.'

Klein's face was suddenly contorted in anguish and despair 'Dead? Are you sure? I only received news from him the other day, how did he die? Was it his heart?'

'No Mr Klein,' I said as innocently as I could, 'apparently he was the victim of an assassination, it seems he was in fact shot.'

'Shot? Assassination? Oh my God, they finally got to him then, poor Ernst.'

'Mr Klein,' Nadine spoke for the first time. 'Who are they? We have unfortunately been caught up in this tragic event whilst not fully understanding what the hell is going on and the reasons for his death.'

I then added, 'I'm very sorry Mr Klein but we must also confess that we were actually sent to kill you too, although it's just really through a combination of bad luck and bad decisions, we find ourselves in the unfortunate position of being killers much against our will and better judgement. We too are the victims here and our lives and the lives of our families have been threatened if we didn't carry out these orders. We came to you not to kill you as instructed but to try to find out just whom is responsible for this apparently senseless slaughter.'

Before Klein could respond, Nadine once more cut in 'What Bob here says is true, we are reluctant assassins, we just want to know the truth of who is behind this crazy situation. I don't take any death lightly Mr Klein and I appreciate that this guy Hoffman was a friend of yours but for all the crimes he committed when he was in the Stasi, I can't really say that I'm sorry for his death for it was far quicker than he delivered to many of his victims.'

At this statement, Mr Klein's face turned from sorrow to anger 'Mr Hoffman in the Stasi? 'Where the hell did you get that information from? Ernst was in fact a victim of that brutal regime; he was imprisoned by them on some jumped-up charge of espionage and spent twelve years in cells suffering sometimes brutal treatment to include starvation and torture too dreadful to even speak about. Ernst was only released at the collapse of the East German state and was then sent to a West German prison on more false charges for another seven years all spent in solitary confinement. He was never afforded a public trial to defend himself or even the luxury of a lawyer to represent him, in fact the West Germans were as bad if not worse than their East German counterparts. Ernst was an opponent of communism and fascism, he was a pacifist, a peace-loving man whose only aim was to expose the organisation behind all this misery to the world. Poor, dear Ernst, so they finally got him after all these years just as he knew they would.'

Nadine reached out and briefly grasped his hand 'Mr Klein, we are so very sorry for the loss of your friend and also for getting the wrong impression about his life and times, obviously we have been fed completely false information by this organisation. But please enlighten us, who exactly are they, who is behind all this mayhem?'

Klein looked at her directly and in a more measured tone said 'They are known by several names, one being as the Illuminati and also as the 3901 which numerals were said to have been carved on the coffin of Rameses the second. Indeed, they originated maybe as far back as the ancient Egyptians, certainly they were an organised force by the Middle Ages, very influential in Spain and then Bavaria, members of this highly secret organisation were thought to be anyone who was anyone at that time, Emperors, Monarchs, Lords and Magnates, Churchmen and even philosophers. They continued to grow their power in more recent times and were linked by rumour to such diverse organisations as the Nazi party and the Ku Klux Klan. They are the most secret of secret organisations, their members are completely unknown to the general public and possibly even to each other, their laws and rituals have never been disclosed, unlike the Masons for instance who are an open book compared to the 3901.'

'They are the modern Princes of darkness, the horsemen of the apocalypse and the self-appointed supreme arbiters of every human soul. They are the anti-Christs, the non-believers who deride religion and who trade souls in pursuit of retaining their overwhelming influence on world events. Their power has no boundaries and with it they can accomplish virtually anything that they want. No-one knows how many they number, it could be scores or it could be single figures but their secrecy is absolute. In all the centuries of their existence nobody has ever been able to name a single one though many have tried.'

'They are thought to be behind most of the tragedies in history, wars, famines, plagues and anything else which has caused suffering to mankind. They have raised some dictators to power, deposed others, won or lost elections and controlled the cost and availability of anything needed for the survival of the human race like energy, food, water and even the weather. They hold sway over the money markets worldwide and they are worth trillions of dollars, pounds and Euros and could bankrupt any country including the USA. if they so desired.'

'They are rumoured to have been behind more recent events like 911 and the Covid outbreak, anyone in the know is fully aware that a Chinese laboratory or indeed a fresh meat market were very unlikely to have been the cause of the pandemic and it was another case where profits of hundreds of millions of dollars and pounds and virtually every other currency could be made without difficulty. These people have unlimited power and can influence every aspect of life in every country and it was this organisation that dear Ernst was working against and the reasons why they had him firstly imprisoned and now killed. He was getting very close to being actually able to name names and his last message to me contained a long list of suspects and he was going to hopefully confirm some names at the beginning of next month when we had planned to meet. The poor man has now taken those possible revelations to his grave.'

'Not necessarily Mr Klein, after all a list of possible candidates for the leadership sounds as promising as anything anyone else has ever produced since the start of this organisation hundreds if not thousands of years ago. By the way do you know a certain Tomas Novak?'

'Tomas? Why of course, he, Ernst and I were all working in our own ways on discovering the secrets of the 3901 organisations, he has amassed a huge amount of data and was collating everything supplied by Ernst and me, he was going to attend our final meeting in Berne next month when it was intended to hopefully unveil some names. He too has suffered false imprisonment in his native Czechoslovakia and like Ernst has been in hiding for quite a while. I decided to take the other route and through my piano playing be as public as possible which up until now has appeared to be successful.'

Nadine broke in again 'Mr Klein, you may have got away with it so far taking the public in full view approach but as one who a few days ago was being ordered to kill you, I beg you now to re-consider. They obviously want you silenced and they won't stop until you are. So, I urge you to now take the opposite course of action and return to Germany or wherever you feel safe and find a suitable hiding place until details about this whole corrupt organization are finally made public and the leaders exposed for the criminals they are.'

Klein responded 'I think you may be right my dear, perhaps being brazen and daring them to do their worst is not now the most sensible approach, I have a cousin who lives in Bavaria who rents out a comfortable but remote cottage in the mountains, I shall contact him after I have cried off from this concert by faking ill health. You must give me an email address and a contact number so that we can keep in touch and I can pass you the relevant list just in case, heaven forbid, something untoward happens to me and to dear Tomas. In the meantime, whilst we three are still hale and hearty I insist that you join me in another pot of this quite excellent tea, the scones here are also amazing as you will soon find out.'

With that he summoned a waiter over and in perfect French made the appropriate order for our refreshments.

I half turned from looking at the departing waiter and as I did, I heard what sounded like a muted woosh of air.

When I looked back, Mr Albert Klein was sitting slumped in his chair, his eyes were open and staring and his mouth too was open as if he was about to speak, he looked very relaxed and calm but there was now a small circular hole in the centre of his forehead which was slowly filling with his blood. I reacted quickly, maybe just by instinct, certainly without any forethought and reached for his wrist where the complete lack of a pulse confirmed that this man had played his last concert.

Nadine who had witnessed the whole thing was staring wild eyed at the sight of Klein's lifeless body but had the peace of mind to address me in a loud whisper 'Bob, take cover, you don't know if you are in someone's gunsight right now, please get down.'

'Nadine,' I replied, 'I am sure that whoever did this is an expert shot and if he had wanted to shoot me and indeed you, he would have done so by now. No, it appears for some strange reason that our late friend Mr Klein was the one and only target on this occasion. Having said that I suggest that we head off that waiter who is coming back with our tea and then get the hell out of this hotel, just in case they change their bloody mind?'

Nadine duly intercepted the waiter before he could see the demise of Mr Klein and casually told him that the old man had in fact dropped off to sleep and therefore it would be very nice of the staff not to clear the table but to let him sleep for at least an hour before waking him. This request, accompanied by quite a large denomination Euro note seemed to have the desired effect as the waiter handed the tray to Nadine and then returned to the bar area where he spoke to the other members of staff gesticulating in our direction as he did so.

With a final sorrowful glance at the poor victim, Nadine and I quickly made our way out of the restaurant back to our room and after collecting our belongings exited by the rear fire escape as quickly as we could. Once in the car Nadine produced her mobile phone and started tapping away in earnest to my more than slight irritation.

'What the hell are you doing? For fucks sake let's get the hell out of here, the police will be here soon and they may just ask too many questions which we can't answer.'

'Relax Bob, Klein won't be disturbed for another hour and then by the time the police are called and arrive we will be miles away. I just thought that we should know where we are going. I don't think going to an airport at this stage is a particularly good idea so I'm looking for a nice little place on the coast of Normandy or Brittany where we can hide out for a couple of days before going to London to find Mr Tomas Novak, the one remaining player in this game of chance. After all we have been through, I think we both deserve some time to relax, unwind and plan our next moves.'

'Nadine, that is the best thing I have ever heard you say, I could sleep for a fortnight without even the need for alcohol to be present, I am feeling that exhausted.'

'Poor dear Bob, well sleep you will most certainly have if not for that long a period and we may even open a bottle or two of wine if you behave yourself. Now will you please just give me a few more minutes of silence for me to go through these adverts?'

People trust their eyes above all else – but most people see what they wish to see, or what they believe they should see; not what is really there.

– Zoe Marriott

7
False Hopes

Nadine duly found what was described as a delightful, secluded chic petit chalet with all mod cons and situated just a few yards from a small secluded sandy beach. This charming residence seemed absolutely perfect and was only some ninety miles away, so without further ado we headed straight there, thankfully reaching it without further incident and within just three hours of leaving the murder scene.

The petit chalet was indeed just as described, a small white weather-boarded cottage nestling below some very tall cliffs and within a hop, skip and a jump of the white sandy beach. Inside it was comfortable rather than luxurious with a large bright double bedroom and an ensuite with both bath and shower. The rest of the accommodation was open plan with a small but fully equipped kitchen leading into a cosy lounge where two large sofas and a wood burning fire added to the feeling of warmth and relaxation. Nadine had already arranged with the owners for them to provide us with all the basics to cook tonight's dinner and tomorrow's breakfast and after a long invigorating walk along the coastal pathway I, at Nadine's insistence, wallowed in a warm, restful bath whilst she prepared our simple dinner of steak and salad accompanied by a delightfully light and vibrant rose wine.

'Thanks Nadine, great dinner,' I said as we sat together on one of the comfortable sofas, her head resting closely against my shoulder. 'You're not only a great cold-blooded killer but you can cook a mean steak too, I really admire women who are so multi-talented.'

'Well Bob I am glad that you liked it but don't think that this is a foretaste of things to come, I am a liberated twenty first century woman and I believe in equal rights for everything so you will be doing your share of cooking in the future.'

'Future? So, you think that we have a future? Could you really see yourself involved with a much older, unfit, overweight guy with a drink problem?'

'Bob, over the last few days I have grown to love you as a person, yes you are no oil painting and most self-respecting attractive, younger woman wouldn't be attracted to you in any way, but this one is and I am willing if you are to give this relationship a go? All of course depending if we both get out of this alive. If we do, as I firmly believe one way or another we will, then I would love to settle down with you, maybe in a little cottage on the coast just like this one, maybe even somewhere in England?'

I was absolutely thrilled that this gorgeous, young, intelligent Lady was envisaging a future with me but I hadn't told her that even if we somehow got out of the present predicament, I still didn't have that much time left to enjoy what I am sure would be a wonderful relationship. I had to tell her, had to bite the bullet now before it was too late and my courage failed me.

'Nadine, there is something very important that you should know about me.'

'Bob, what is it? Why suddenly so serious? you're scaring me now, what the hell is this important matter? You're not married or anything like that are you?'

'No Nadine, nothing so horrendous as that, I just have cancer, a very rare form for which there is no cure, I have been told by the specialists that without treatment I may have two maybe even three years left to live if I am very lucky and up to five years with intensive treatment.'

'My God Bob and you have kept this from me the whole time we've been in this mess? So, are you on medication?'

'I take two pills twice a day and that's all, I have been told to lay off red meat, sugar and alcohol too.'

'Which is just what we had for dinner, if you had told me before I cooked, I could have prepared something else.'

‘Oh Nadine, I really enjoyed that dinner, do you think that a plate of just salad washed down by tap water would have tasted as tenth as good? Please don’t spoil this idyllic little break, I haven’t felt as happy and relaxed in years and it’s all down to you.’

‘Okay Bob, no more lecturing I promise you but you say that there is some form of treatment available that could help you to live longer?

‘Yes Nadine, if I undergo radiotherapy treatment, they say that I might reasonably expect to add two more years to my life expectancy and they have also intimated that there are several new exciting trials taking place for my type of cancer which might, just might be available in time for me.’

‘Well then, there’s no argument about what to do, you must have whatever treatment they can give you and we can both pray that in the meantime they find a cure or at least some drugs that can extend your time on earth even longer.’

‘That’s exactly the way I was going to go but now I have met you that is all changed.’

‘All changed – how so?’ said Nadine in a very worried voice.

‘Because darling, being with you here close like this has given me an entirely different outlook on my life. Yes of course, I’m in no real hurry to die and the thought of a couple of extra years and even the prospect of some kind of cure are extremely tempting but…'

'But what?'

'But now I have realised that I would have to start treatment sooner rather than later and that would involve numerous courses of radiotherapy leading to frequent and prolonged bouts of intense pain and sickness meaning that yes, I was prolonging my life but gaining quantity of years at the cost of quality of living. You may say that you would stick by me and support me come what may but being a nursemaid twenty-four seven to someone who is in constant discomfort would not be what you signed up for and I would not let you do it. No, now I have met you I would much rather have whatever time is left to me by your side, hopefully in good health for most of that time and darling we can pack as much excitement and happiness into those few years as most people do in a long lifetime. We can travel to parts of the world other people can only dream of and have such a wondrous journey together that, if in that time no cure has been found, we won't be angry and we won't be sad as we would have lived as few people have.'

Nadine was by this time trying desperately and failing to keep her feelings in check as tears streamed down her cheeks and I had to dab ineffectively to stem the flow with a wad of paper tissues from the box our hosts had thoughtfully provided.

‘Bob.’ She said in a choking voice ‘I have only just found you and I sure as hell don’t even want to think about losing you and it’s one heck of a decision to make and believe me, I can see the arguments on both sides of this dilemma. When do you have to make up your mind what you are going to do?’

‘I have nine days before my appointment is scheduled to take place though let’s face it, I may not be alive to even make that date so the decision may well never have to be made. However, if you agree, then I’m most certainly leaning heavily towards opting for no treatment and a full but shorter future.’

‘Well Bob we still have some time to think about this and you’re right, let’s get ourselves out of this scrape in one piece first and then we’ll know if there’s a future for either of us. Speaking of the immediate task at hand I’ve decided to give you the passport, half the cash and details of Mr Thomas Novak, just in case anything happens to me, you must carry on and try to find him or all this would have been in vain. Not that I think it will ever come to that Bob, I have a feeling, call it woman’s intuition if you like, that we will both get out of this scrape and if we can’t live happily ever after, we can at least live a lot longer together. The day after tomorrow we will drive to Brest airport and board a flight to London, we may as well use our own names now as I don’t think that it’s going to make any difference as they know all our aliases better than we do. I would rather not die as Mrs Shirley Smith if I have to die at all.'

Despite the lovely glowing sunset we retired early and that night we made the sweetest lovemaking I have ever encountered, not frantic and unbridled like our previous tryst but gentle and caring yet passionate in its own way too. Our two bodies entwined as one for what seemed like an eternity as we both expressed our love and desire for each other in the way only true lovers can.

The next morning, I was awakened by the early morning sun peeping through the half-opened blinds as the new day dawned rich and full of promise. I gazed with wonder at the sleeping figure of Nadine, her glossy mane of hair covering the pillow and her angelic face looking so beautiful and contented. I must have stared at her for some considerable time all the while thinking how could a gorgeous, intelligent young Lady like her fall for an old has-been, more like never-been, as me? I couldn't work out a satisfactory answer at all, maybe it was just pity or a case of opposites attracting. I gave up these thoughts pretty quickly and prayed silently to God let me just be glad of this time and hopefully of the even better times to come.

We had the perfect breakfast of hot strong coffee accompanied by toasted hunks of local seeded granary bread smothered in bright yellow butter and homemade blueberry preserve and supported by fresh local figs and juicy red grapes. We discussed our course of action for this, our last day in this idyllic location, and decided to explore the coastline by walking along the beach towards the next bay some three miles away.

‘Oh Bob, as I was preparing breakfast, they announced on the radio that the well know piano virtuoso Mr Albert Klein had died suddenly from a heart attack just before he was due to perform at the Elysee Palace for the President.’

‘A heart attack?’ I said in disbelief. ‘How the hell could they manage that? These people it seems can do anything they like and get away with it, the sooner they are named and shamed the better place the entire world will be.’

‘Bob, it also means that we have to be extra careful in this the home straight, let’s keep our eyes peeled, even on this walk and be as prepared as we can be for anything at any time.’

We had only just stepped off the small balcony area to go back into the kitchen when Nadine froze and said ‘Bob, don’t make it too obvious but take a look up there on the hill and tell me that I’m wrong, that I’m seeing things.’ I slowly turned full circle and glanced in the direction Nadine had indicated. Sure enough, a man was standing in the grass near the top of the rise and seemed to be staring intently in our direction through a pair of what looked like heavy duty service binoculars. The hairs at the back of my neck most definitely stood firmly to attention and the phrase my blood ran cold seemed all of a sudden to be extremely apt.

'It's them for sure Nadine, they've somehow tracked us down and God knows what those bastards intend to do now but let's not hang around to find out, I think we should leave immediately.' So, for the third time in a few days, we packed our meagre belongings in haste, loaded up the car and headed for the main road to Brest airport and hopefully this time to freedom.

Nadine gunned the old warhorse of a car as quickly as she could as we finally left that lovely place far behind and eventually made our way through the maze of country lanes onto a minor but still quite pacey road with no sign of being followed and our full attention focused on the last leg of our long journey home.

I didn't see the open backed lorry that emerged from the left side junction at such great speed until the very last minute and I only think that I shouted at Nadine in panic but then everything seemed to go into slow motion mode and I was only dimly aware of the sound of the dashboard and front fascia of the car somehow crumbling into pieces in front of me then suddenly I felt a tremendous pain in my chest and then mercifully the darkness engulfed me totally.

I awoke only due to the sharp bright light that some moron was shining directly into my eyes. 'Oh Mr Owen, so glad that you are back with us, parlez vous Francais?' I must have mumbled that at this stage I couldn't even understand the King's English because the man just seemed to disappear and I fell back into a deep, deep sleep. Later, much later or so it felt to me, the man reappeared with two others all wearing white coats with the statutory stethoscopes dangling from their necks. 'Mr Owen, we are very pleased that you are awake and with it,' said the taller of the three with that trace of a French accent that for some unfathomable reason, women seem to find so endearing. 'You have had a very serious accident and you are a very, very lucky man to be alive let alone escape with some broken ribs, a broken nose and some lacerations to your arms and legs. According to the emergency services you seemed to have hit that tree with some force and without the modern luxury of airbags in your ancient vehicle, all I can say is someone must have been watching over you.'

'What about Nadine?' I asked, my concern rising by the second, why hadn't they mentioned her, was she badly injured, or worse still? 'Is she okay?'

'Nadine?' The middle one said in an even more exaggerated accent 'Who is Nadine?'

'Why the bloody driver of course, my partner, the younger woman, long hair.' I faltered as they all looked at me in that dubious way that people look when they are hearing total nonsense.

'Mr Owen,' the first one said in a very condescending voice. 'You were the only occupant of the car when the emergency services arrived, you were found in the driving seat with the steering wheel crushing you against the seat and apparently, they had to cut you free which took some considerable time and effort. I think maybe the severe concussion you suffered may have temporarily affected your memory, don't worry this is quite common in cases like yours, total rest is what you need and then you will see all will be fine.'

'Listen.' I shouted. Don't you understand? Nadine was with me, she was driving, she was the one on the driver's seat, she.' I stopped as suddenly, even in my groggy state I realised the awful truth, 3901 had somehow arranged this, they had taken her, dead or alive and engineered me into the driver's seat and staged the collision with the tree, the bastards had got us just when we thought we had escaped them.

The Doctors looked at each other again and I knew that they didn't believe me. 'Just get some rest Mr Owen,' one said. 'The sedative we have given you should help but don't hesitate to push this button if you feel you need some more pain control, otherwise sleep is the best medicine for you right now. We will try to ensure that the Police leave you alone at least for a while.'

The Police of course, I hadn't even thought about the possible consequences of this ridiculous so-called accident – I didn't have any insurance, and had no idea if that old car was covered by any MOT or whatever the French equivalent was, supposing they said it was dangerous driving too? My head was already thumping, my sides felt like they'd been kicked by a mule and my vision was blurry at best but somehow, I had to get out of this nightmare before it was too late. However, even I realised that I couldn't go anywhere yet in my present state and after fighting unsuccessfully to stay awake I drifted back into dreamland and peace.

Sometime later, was it hours or even days? I was awakened by another unfamiliar voice. 'Mr Owen we are very sorry to disturb you but unfortunately there are some questions that we need to ask you with regards to the accident you have been involved in.' One of the two men in uniform spoke these words in the best form of English yet with absolutely no trace of a French accent, indeed he sounded like he had almost certainly been born somewhere deep in stockbroker Surrey.

'I am very sorry Officer but at present the entire thing is just a blur, I can't even remember getting into the car, let alone driving it or where I was going, my only very vague recollection is a lorry coming out of a side road and heading straight at me, then everything is blank after that.'

'Well, Mr Owen, according to our colleagues in road traffic operations, there wasn't any other vehicle involved in the crash, your car appears to have left the road for no apparent reason and hit a large Oak tree head-on thus causing the damage to itself and you by this action. Are you positive that you can't recall any more details?'

'No, I'm sorry but although I am trying very hard to remember it's all a complete black hole at present.' I wasn't really lying as the reasons for the accident and exactly how I had ended up in the driver's seat of a car wrapped around an enormous tree were indeed completely unknown to me. Luckily, I was saved the need for further explanations when one of the three Doctors who had been with me earlier suddenly appeared and ushered the protesting Policemen away, shouting at them something in French that I couldn't understand but which seemed to do the trick as they both rather unhappily disappeared out of the room. When the Doctor returned to my bedside he said 'They just won't give up I'm afraid Mr Owen, they want some answers and some documentation from you and they will be back tomorrow when hopefully you will be feeling a lot better. I regret that you will also then be receiving a visit from the hospital admin department to sort out your personal health insurance and arrange for your onward journey, back to England I presume? Anyway, that's for tomorrow, for today it's just rest and pain control, so I will bid you good day until we do our rounds in the morning.'

I lay back on the pillows and closed my eyes, what a fucking mess I thought, yet more reasons not to hang about this place and I determined only to wait until the evening shift came on to the ward and maybe then I could try to mingle with the visitors as they left at around eight pm.

So, still feeling like death warmed up, as the changeover to night staff occurred at seven o'clock, I got up, with great difficulty, from my bed and checked in my bedside locker where my personal belongings had been placed. Luckily my jacket, though now torn and bloody, was in the locker so at least I had cash and, what was more important my passport which was still in the pocket and seemed to have escaped the violence of the crash. Unfortunately, the same could not be said of my jeans and shirt which were literally torn to shreds and very bloodstained and had been placed in a plastic bag together though Lord knows why. I had no choice but to put on the suit that we had purchased what seemed like an age ago, without a shirt it looked pretty stupid and even more so when the only footwear were my torn and bloodied trainers. However, I had no real choice so I tried to swagger out of the room and down the corridor into the front entrance as if I was one very cool dude. My swagger soon turned to a stagger as I approached the information area where the middle-aged woman behind the screen almost recoiled as I stood swaying in front of her. Seeing my reflection staring back at me from the highly polished glass I could understand why: apart from the almost comical appearance of my attire I was also standing sporting two black and swollen eyes, a heavy plaster across my nose and numerous cuts and bruises over the rest of my face.

She excitedly gave me what seemed like a real telling off but as it was all in French it didn't really matter as I couldn't hardly understand one word in six of what she said. When I offered the old justification for my ignorance 'English,' that one word somehow seemed enough and she just repeated 'ah English' as if that entirely explained my appearance. With a mixture of schoolboy French, hand gestures and very slowly spoken English I managed, eventually, to convey to her that I needed a cab as soon as possible. When pressed for my destination and thinking of the Police questioning her tomorrow, I said, 'Brest Railway Station,' which seemed to satisfy her and within ten minutes a sleek Mercedes pulled to a halt outside the entrance and the driver announced that he had come to pick up the crazy Englishman which I rightly presumed meant me. Once in the cab the driver, after doing a double-take over my appearance, asked me in broken English, 'So you want to go to Brest Railway Station?'

‘No,’ I replied, ‘I’ve changed my mind, please take me to Brest Airport.’ And with a shrug of his shoulders and a ‘Oui Monsieur’ off we set.

When we got to the airport, I paid the driver and included a very large tip so that if asked he would tell anyone that he had indeed dropped me off at the station. Once inside the airport terminal I purchased a ticket for the next flight to Heathrow which was taking off in three hours’ time and then made my way to the nearest shop in the concourse where I managed to purchase a shirt, jeans and jumper which enabled me to change in the public toilets, clean-up the trainers and to leave the suit in the nearest rubbish bin.

I then went through security and the customs checks with only the odd startled glance from the officials at the sight of me, maybe thinking I was something to do with the football fans that were thronging the airport after a recent match between the national teams of France and England. I was grateful for their presence as I somehow felt safe that no-one, not even the 3901, would dare to carry out an attack with so many people present. That didn’t however stop me eying anyone suspiciously who even looked vaguely in my direction as I made my way airside where I purchased the largest box of the strongest painkillers that I could find and then went to the café where I bought a large bowl of onion soup with some half stale hunks of white bread and a plate of French fries covered in mayonnaise, my first food of the day, all washed down with a large brandy. Eventually my flight was called and feeling refreshed and more relaxed but still walking very unsteadily and with a head throbbing like the jet turbos spinning round on the aeroplane's wings I boarded for the short flight home.

Many things are not as they seem:
The worst things in life never are.

– Jim Butcher

8
Endgame

The journey proved to be uneventful although my hopes of a peaceful flight home where I could drift off for a well needed sleep proved illusory as the football fans not only indulged in over consumption of alcohol but also decided that they should sing bawdy songs for the entire length of the journey.

When we landed at Heathrow and after clearing customs, I did feel a whole lot better at being back in England, somehow it felt safer although I knew only too well that I was as likely to be killed here as anywhere else I had recently been to.

I had made up my mind on the plane that I would contact brother George, not to ask for police protection or even to tell him my story but just to find out if by a miracle he could find out if Nadine was still alive. There was a faint hope that if she had survived, she may have contacted him as he was the only person I had really mentioned when telling her my tales of woe that I had endured at the hands of Mr Mystery and his cronies.

George was home when I rang but was quite put out by being woken from his slumbers at midnight to be asked by his obviously drunken wastrel of a brother if a woman called Nadine, a friend whom I had known only for a very long week or so, had been in touch. Answering firmly in the negative and after imploring me once again to give up the booze for good a disgruntled George ended the call.

Uncertain, without Nadine's flair for planning, what to do next I decided that sleep was the first port of call so I booked myself into one of the airport hotels. Once in my room I took a handful of painkillers and fell into bed to sleep the sleep of the damned and the dead for what hopefully would be for ever. In the event it wasn't for ever, in fact despite my mental and physical exhaustion I only managed sporadic bouts of sleep as the pain of my ribs made it virtually impossible to get my body into a comfortable position for any length of time.

In the morning after painfully showering and dressing very slowly and carefully I went to the hotel restaurant and devoured a huge full English with all the trimmings and several cups of coffee. I still felt far from my normal self but knew that I didn't have time to recuperate as I should have, I had to find Mr Tomas Novak and hopefully together we could approach the authorities with the information supplied to him by his two deceased colleagues. I then somehow had to find out the truth about Nadine's disappearance and whether she was indeed as dead as they were.

I looked once more at the address that Nadine had given me for Thomas Novak and was slightly puzzled that it was a flat in South West London which hardly the most salubrious location for such a learned man to hang out in. Maybe though that is exactly why he was there, maybe in his mind this was the last place anyone would look for him. I got the underground to Balham station then went to the local cab office and gave them the address. 'Are you sure you want to go here?' The decidedly portly man said though the glass partition. 'It's a bit of a rough area. Mind you, if you don't mind me saying, from the state you're in you look like you've been somewhere even worse.' I smiled at him as best I could manage and through gritted teeth said the classic line 'you should see the other feller.'

I made the cab driver drop me off a couple of hundred yards from the address so I could look around the area and I could see exactly what the cab office man had meant, it was indeed the kind of place where you expected there to be trouble at any minute with abandoned cars, boarded windows and that menacing air of desolation that only inner-city areas can generate. There was a collection of high-rise buildings on this rundown estate and our man lived at the very top of the middle block of five.

I approached the entrance over some broken glass that crunched underfoot and when I reached the battered front door I was surprised to find, amongst all this mayhem, that it was still securely locked. It proved impervious to my pathetic attempts to force it open, groaning as I did so from the discomfort in my ribs. I muttered a prayer of forgiveness for all my many past sins and slowly pressed the buzzer for the top flat which amazingly also appeared to be in working order as the buzzing noise vibrated around the strangely silent entrance lobby. There was no reply so I pressed long and hard again but to no avail. I therefore took my life in my hands and starting with the flat below, pressed every buzzer on the keypad but either no-one was in or if they were, they weren't answering. I stepped away and was just about to retire down the road to consider my options when a female voice shouted out, 'Hey, hold on don't go,' and a young female clad only in a short dressing gown and a pair of high heeled pink mule type slippers opened the door.

'Hi there, are you Jake?' she said in a harsh voice which somehow sounded much older than her adolescent looks.

'No darling,' I said, 'but I wish I was, I'm just here to visit my old friend Thomas but thanks for letting me in.' With that I pushed a ten-pound note in her hand and strode past her to the lift.

Of course, the lift was out of order which I only knew because it didn't respond to my pushing every single button on its control panel.

'It's not working,' the young girl said, 'hasn't been for ages. Would you like to come in for a cup of tea and a chat and visit your friend later?'

'No thanks,' I responded, 'I have to see my friend urgently, maybe some other time?' and made straight for the stairs.

Walking up so many flights of stairs in my usual condition would probably have proved challenging but now with the chronic pain from my ribs and the various aches and pains over most of the rest of my body it was more, much more than just challenging and several times I had to stop in order to regain my breath and to gain temporary relief from the constant jarring of my limbs. I don't know how long it took me but eventually I stumbled onto the landing of the top floor.

It was then that I immediately realised something was wrong, very wrong as the door to the flat numbered thirty-six was ajar and I could plainly hear the sound of a loud television or maybe radio emanating from within. It didn't take a Hercules Poirot to work out that this just wasn't right and I wondered if the best course of action would be to turn around and leave before it was too late. However, if nothing else, the thought of descending those steps again without knowing what might or might not have happened put some fresh courage into my weakening resolve and pushing open the door I entered the flat.

The first thing that struck me was that the lights were on and the hallway was therefore very well-lit and with the noise that was emanating from inside the flat it was feeling surreal and very creepy. I looked inside the doorway of the first room I came to and there laying on the bed illuminated by the brightness of the bedroom lights and the bright sunlight steaming through the opened curtains was Tomas Novak. He was fully clothed and looked for all the world that he was sleeping but his face had a mottled slightly bluish colour and when I felt his wrist it was cold, clammy and lifeless. I tried to close his open staring eyes but they refused to budge as if someone had super-glued them open, so I pulled the bed cover up over his entire body in order to afford him at least a modicum of decency.

Looking around the bedroom it was obvious that the room had been thoroughly searched and that the searchers had not made any attempts to conceal their mission as the contents of drawers and cupboards covered the floor where they had been examined and then discarded. Retracing my steps out of the room I walked down the narrow eerie hallway and found the same scenes of destruction in every room including the tiny kitchen where even the sugar pot had been emptied of its contents. Reaching the lounge at the end of the hallway, I turned off the television which had been left on at full volume and then pulled aside the heavy curtain that covered the large picture window and gazed down to street level, but all was quiet, whoever had caused the murder had it seemed long gone,

I turned all the lights off and closed the front door behind me before making the long but slightly less painful descent of the staircase. When I reached ground level, I thought it best to exit by the rear door but just as my hand reached out to grab the handle a police car silently glided up on the road outside. I didn't wait to see if they were heading for the flats but made my way to the front entrance and there on the road beyond the rubbish strewn, lawned gardens was parked another police car with the occupants just alighting from the vehicle. I ducked back into the shelter of the lobby and having little other option banged as hard as I could on the nearest flat door.

The young female from our earlier encounter eventually opened the door partway to reveal a door chain between me and safety. 'Oh it's you again, your friend not in or have you changed your mind about that cup of tea? She smiled as she said this last part.

'No, he's not in,' I lied, 'and I'm afraid there are some bad men out to get me, if you can just let me in for a few minutes, I'll make it worth your while?'

'Well, why didn't you say before? In you come Mister, if you're paying, stay as long as you like but my Tony usually gets back around six so it's best that you're not still here then.'

She released the chain and just as I heard the main front door open, I stepped inside and silently closed the door to her flat. I then heard footsteps going past and minutes later some cursing as they must have discovered the lift was out of order. I couldn't be sure that all the policemen, if they were indeed policemen, had entered the building so I asked her, 'Are there any other ways out of here?'

'Yes Mister, there's the rear door leading to the patio area but if the bad men are outside, they will see you or you could get out of the bedroom window, there you'll be shielded by the bin sheds and you should be able to sneak into the next block of flats opposite.'

Thanking her profusely and placing a wad of cash into her eager hands I took her advice and exited through the bedroom window where indeed my movements were concealed from anyone watching at either of the entrances. Reaching the next block, I rang every buzzer until someone got fed up with the incessant noise I was making and opened the front door. I walked up and down the lobby observing the police cars until after around twenty minutes they both drove off and giving it another ten minutes or so I slipped out and eventually made my way back to the station.

I approached my home with more than a little trepidation the awful memories of my last stay there still vivid in my mind. However, I was pleasantly surprised to find that instead of any anticipated death and destruction there was just a pile of bills and junk mail awaiting me. All seemed quiet and somehow reassuring after the tumult of the recent past. I took a long soak in the bath which seemed to do wonders for my poor aching ribs and after ordering a Chinese food delivery which I ate ravenously accompanied by a few beers and a generous measure of brandy, I fell into my bed which I had never missed so much in my entire life.

It must have been several hours later, perhaps three in the morning when something caused me to stir from my well-deserved slumbers and I slowly opened my eyes to be confronted by the figure of Nadine standing at the foot of my bed. However, as I instantly realised, this wasn't Nadine as I had last seen her, sitting beside me in the car, looking radiant and laughing as we shared that happy trip to the airport. No, this Nadine looked very much like I did when I came round in hospital, both her eyes were blackened and her face and arms bore marks of many wounds, some superficial and some looking more serious, there was a large patch of bright red blood showing through her top where it looked like she had sustained a very nasty injury.

'Bob,' she said in a faltering voice, 'why did you leave me? Where did you go?'

'Nadine, I didn't leave you darling, there was a crash in the car and the next thing I knew I was coming out of a coma in hospital and they said that there was no sign of you.'

Her voice rose more urgently 'Liar, you left me, left me there in that car to die.'

Before I had the chance to answer she had disappeared and in her place was the figure of Hoffman the would-be monk. 'Mr Owen,' he said with a strong German accent. 'Why did you allow me to be killed when we were complete strangers, what had I ever done to you?'

I didn't, couldn't answer this question, my mouth was frozen in fear and then the vision of Hoffman was replaced by that of Abbot Ricci still with that puzzled expression on his face exactly as it was when he turned to see me in that room.

'Mr Owen, why did you allow a peaceful man of God to be slaughtered in cold blood, you will be damned for all eternity.' The figure was immediately replaced by that of Albert Klein, so white-faced with that perfect round bullet hole in his forehead and just a small drop of dried blood to show that the shot had caused injury.

'Mr Owen, you led them to me, if it wasn't for your harebrained chase across Europe, I would still be alive, my blood is on your hands.' He too faded away and in his place I saw the mottled, frightened face of Tomas Novak.

'Mr Owen, without you I would still be alive, you led them to me, my death is down to you.' I lay there helpless, motionless as one more vision appeared before me, a young woman this time, vaguely familiar, a face from my past that I had tried to wipe from my memory. 'Captain Bob Owen, how come you are still living when so many good young men are dead? Is your conscience not haunted by the memories of those brave souls whom you tortured, maimed and killed in the name of your Queen?' Linda Boyle, sister of the two young men we killed way back in nineteen eighty-nine during the troubles of Northern Ireland.

My body eventually started to react and began shaking violently as my tortured brain tried to figure out the meaning of this nightmare, horrified by the content but also profoundly relieved that it was just a dream even if a mind zapping one that I never ever wanted to experience again. I rose shakily from my bed and downed a couple of large gulps of brandy which, temporarily at least, did have a calming influence on my shattered nerves. I was in absolutely no mood to return to bed and switched on the television and sat watching an ancient Gary Coper movie until the dawn finally broke through the open curtains of the room.

My temporary peace of mind was rudely interrupted by the buzzing of my phone as a text message was received, from George, a little cryptic but asking me to meet him at the Rose and Crown pub in Crayford at eleven thirty as he had some important news for me. Important news indeed, hopefully about Nadine but it was very ominous that he didn't say good news. I took my time and fixed myself a very sad breakfast of toast made from defrosted white bread and eggs that were probably way past their sell-by date, I didn't have the courage to check but they tasted okay although I must admit that my appetite had been somewhat diminished by the events of the night.

I made my way by bus and train to the pub and arrived just before the appointed time and due to the fact that it had only just opened and I was the only customer in view I guessed I was the first of the day. However, as I approached the bar the young-looking guy behind the bar politely asked 'Mr Owen?' and when I replied in the affirmative informed me that my brother was waiting in the beer garden and he had even bought me a drink. Well, I thought, things were at last looking up, either there was indeed good news about Nadine or he had got another promotion and wanted to show-off the fact to his layabout older brother.

I walked into the garden which was very quickly warming from the mid-morning sun and walked towards the only occupied table right at the farthest end from the pub door. 'George this is a surprise,' I started to say when the man turned round and a very familiar voice greeted me 'Why hello Bob, nice to see you, how are you? You do look rather the worse for wear, have you been involved in a fight or something?'

That was really the final straw that broke the camel's back, shouting like a madman I hurled myself at the perplexed looking Mr Mystery and took great satisfaction in landing a good few body blows until two burly men appeared out of nowhere and literally tore me from my opponent. 'Leave him alone now boys.' He said breathing heavily but sitting back quite calmly in the chair. 'Wait over there near the door, I don't think Mr Owen will be trying any more heroics, will you Bob?'

'You bastard,' I screamed still in a rage. 'You and your so-called secret society have caused the deaths of many innocent people and nearly mine too, what the fuck is this all about and where the hell is Nadine, have you got her, is she still alive?'

'Calm down Bob, you are getting very close to coronary territory, firstly neither I or any of my colleagues would have had to kill anyone if you had done your job properly. You and your accomplice acted more like Laurel and Hardy than the cold-blooded killers we thought we had hired. You had the simple task of eliminating one sick, old man by lethal injection and what happened? You left a scene behind you that looked like the battle of the Alamo, blood and bodies everywhere. You ask about Nadine, well Bob as an old soldier yourself, you know that in every unsuccessful operation there are casualties, even we can't protect everyone all the time. Look on the bright side, you are alive and kicking and a few broken ribs and minor abrasions aside, in very rude health. Also, when you check your bank balance you will find that despite your colossal failure a substantial bonus has been deposited there'

'A bonus? A bribe to keep me quiet more like, you know that I could go to my…'

Mr Mystery interrupted 'to your brother? Oh yes, he's a middle ranking officer in the Met. Bob, don't you yet understand that your brother could be the Chief Constable, the Home Secretary or the United Nations Secretary General and it wouldn't make one iota of difference, no-one would believe one word of your very tall tale. There are three men who are now dead who were causing us a very minor irritation, check the records and you will see that they all died of natural causes. Before you say anything about exhumation of the bodies, the first two have already been cremated and in the case of Mr Novak, a football team of the best pathologists in the world would only return a verdict of death by natural causes. Now the reason why you are still alive and indeed rewarded may well be because you are not worth the bother of killing, after all you caused the desired diversion, you served your purpose though not quite as it was originally envisaged. Why you have been quite so lucky I must confess is something of a mystery to me, without exception people who have displayed your level of incompetence would be classed as traitors by the organisation and would suffer a traitor's fate. The reason you are being spared is therefore beyond normal comprehension unless they are content to just let that horrible disease you're suffering from kill you. More likely they want you to stay alive at least for a while to set an example of failure not by killing you in the accustomed manner but by making you suffer an uncertain future. Every time the phone rings or there's a knock at the door you will die a little bit at a time. You won't know if it's an Amazon delivery or a much more unwelcome visit from an assassin, a competent assassin. If I were you Bob, I would think myself lucky and walk away a free man, get on with your miserable existence, drink yourself to death, you have the funds to do so. Forget all this ever happened, don't let yourself become another minor irritation.'

‘Well maybe, just maybe I would like to carry on being a minor irritation as you call it, maybe I’m not prepared to say thank you for dragging me across Europe and seeing people killed a few yards from me, perhaps I want the whole world to wake-up to the seriousness of the situation, to your power and to your very evil designs on mankind. I know that in your Organisation’s warped vision of reality me and millions of other ordinary people like me don’t have a voice let alone any influence but sooner rather than later that will change and you will all get your just desserts. In the meantime, I’m certainly not in the mood to thank you for my apparent good fortune in still being alive and much less to be eternally grateful for cancelling or indeed postponing my ultimate demise.’

‘Bob, that is all very noble and I am sure you believe in every mealy-mouthed platitude you just uttered but you must get real, you can never win, you’re tilting at windmills without a lance, without hope and without a chance of success. Believe it or not Bob, I quite like you but I do hope for your sake that our paths never cross again, not that it would be me in person you understand. So farewell Bob, take care and don’t ever get greedy again. Settle for what you’ve got, it’s a lot better than those others have, they only have a grave, just remember that.’

He turned on his heel and walked away from me but then halfway to the door, he stopped and retraced his steps until he was almost touching me, 'One last thing Bob, just reflect that the one lesson you surely must have learned in all this mayhem is that there is no such thing as absolute truth and that nothing is always as it seems.' He then walked to the door and exited the pub garden and hopefully my life.

I sat there for quite some time ruminating on what had just passed between us and indeed on the utter madness of the last fortnight. Despite the fact that it appears I was out of immediate danger and could indeed resume my life, such as it was, I was still consumed by the feelings of anger and dismay at the pointless loss of lives. Even more so was my sense of grief at the loss of dear, sweet Nadine and though I didn't in any way blame myself for her loss, I was distraught that the best thing that had ever happened to me was now no more. I felt a sense of complete loneliness and abandonment which I was sure could never be overcome. A single, wasted and probably drunken future was all I had to look forward to, my heart ached so much.

As I sat there with these contrasting emotions of guilt and emptiness a sudden voice from behind aroused me from the lethargy of my self-pity.

'Bob, where the hell have you been?'

The End

Other Books by Andy Casey

Curses and Verses (2014) | ISBN 9781784620295

Olly & Me (2020) | ISBN 9781913653439

Reflections (2023) | ISBN 9781800946163

Available worldwide from Amazon and all good bookstores

Find Andy Casey at:

www.andycaseyauthor.com

Facebook @AndyCaseyAuthor

Instagram @andycaseyauthor

TikTok @andycaseyauthor

X @AndyCaseyAuthor

andycaseyauthor@gmail.com

Michael Terence Publishing

Action Bladder Cancer UK

Registered charity no: 1164374

Action Bladder Cancer UK was set up to improve outcomes for bladder cancer patients. Our concern is the low profile of such a common cancer, the lack of awareness amongst the public and health professionals and the lack of critical research funding.

Action
Bladder Cancer UK

Printed in Dunstable, United Kingdom

79477469R00092